SILVER CITY

by

A.J. Lee

This is a work of fiction. Names, characters, places and incidents either are the product of the author's imagination or are used fictitiously, and any resemblance to actual persons, living or dead, events, or locales is entirely coincidental.

Copyright © 2003 by A.J. Lee. All rights reserved.

All rights reserved. No part of this book may be reproduced or transmitted in any form or by any means, electronic or mechanical, including photocopying, recording or by any information storage and retrieval system, without written permission from the author, except for the inclusion of brief quotations in a review.

ISBN, printed edition	0-9746228-4-2
ISBN, PDF edition	0-9746228-5-0

Library of Congress Catalog Number: 2003097879

order@pickuppress.com

Lee, A. J., 1948-
    Silver City / by A.J. Lee.
    p. cm.
    LCCN 2003097879
    ISBN 0-9746228-4-2 (printed ed.)
    ISBN 0-9746228-5-0 (PDF ed.)

    1. Deary, Jacob, 1846-1899—Fiction. 2. Idaho—History—Fiction. 3. Historical fiction. 4. Western stories. I. Title.

PS36123.E3424S55 2004   813'.6
                                  QBI33-1725

Printed in the United States of America
Pickup Press trade paperback / June 2004
Pickup Press • Boise, Idaho

for my wife Sasha

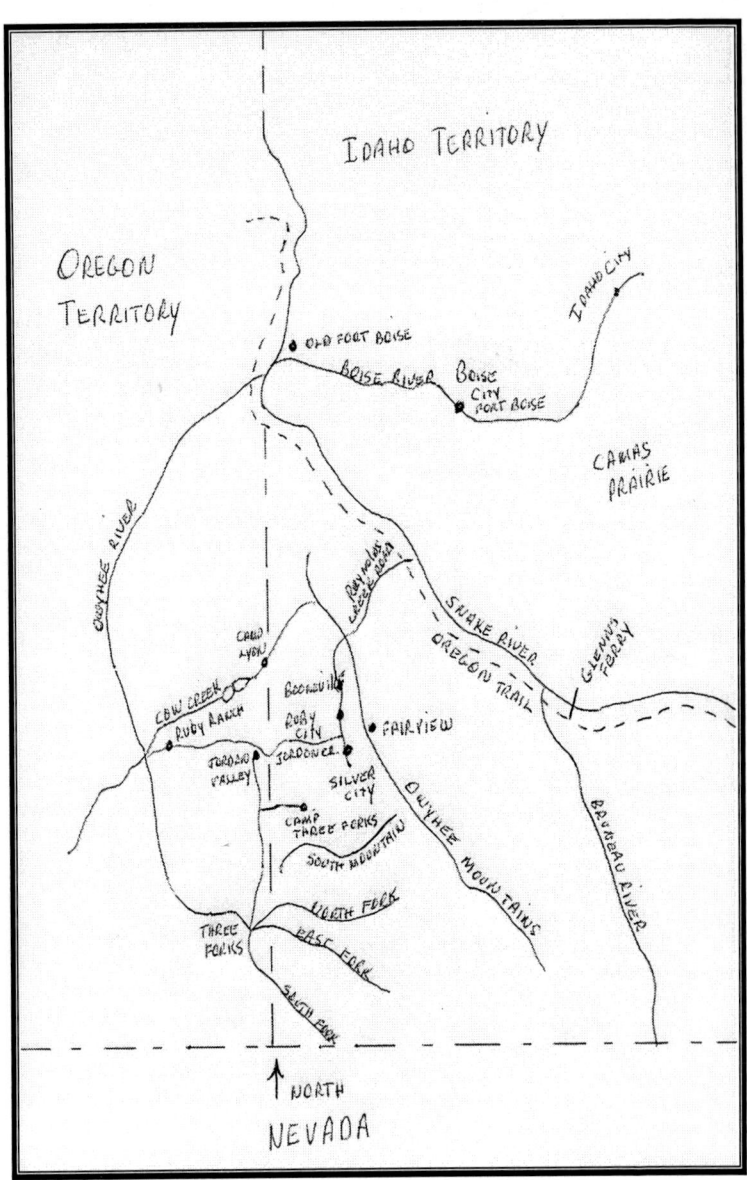

ONE

Under a full moon in June of 1865, Jacob Deary lay motionless in his bedroll. Only the rapid beating of his heart betrayed that he was awake and alert. The still, dead silence woke him, and now he listened for the sound of any movement. Then he heard the faint rustling in the willows near the creek, fifty yards away. The noise was not his picketed horse. Slowly he moved his hand out of the bedroll and onto his revolver. His hand rested on the cold steel with thumb on the hammer and finger on the trigger. He resolved to respond with the next noise.

Again the willows rustled. With one motion, Jacob Deary began to rise and swing the heavy Colt .44 toward the faint noise. Time froze and before he could lock the hammer, Jacob saw a flash from the muzzle and knew his response was late. The 50-caliber ball entered high and right in his chest, burning and slamming him to the ground. His right arm went limp and the revolver fell to the ground. The rifle blast reverberated in his ears.

The moon shone bright and stars filled the night sky. The canyon entrance, willows and sagebrush were coated with moonlight. Jacob lay, stunned and bleeding, his breathing coming in short, shallow bursts.

In the willows, the giant Indian lowered his Mississippi Yager rifle. He knew the shot was true and had struck a lethal blow to the White man. Two braves crouched behind Nampuh, waiting for the signal to move forward from their hiding place.

The three Indians moved out of the willows toward the downed man. They came up and stood over Jacob. One brave drew his knife. The huge dark leader motioned him to stop and directed him to the saddlebags, revolver, and Springfield rifle. Nampuh motioned the other Indian toward the picketed horse. Since the wagon massacre, Nampuh took no more scalps.

Jacob Deary focused and saw the silhouette of a giant man with two smaller figures. He thought, "Is this all a dream?" With all his strength, he tried to rise and attack. His vision narrowed and all sound became distant and seemed to echo. Jacob collapsed. All went black.

Nampuh looked at the young man's face, watching the brief struggle. The Indian was not there to kill. Unknowingly, Jacob Deary had made camp between the infamous Indian Nampuh and the stagecoach.

Nampuh and his braves had come to Reynolds Creek to rob the morning stage from the mining district, which always carried a rich load of gold and silver. This was familiar territory for them. Whites referred to the area as "Massacre Flats". The robbers could jump the stage before it headed out of the valley and up toward the pass, then vanish into the rugged canyon and down the creek. Anyone foolish enough to follow was easily ambushed in the narrow canyon.

Silently, the band of robbers collected the spoils and turned back toward the willows. Unsure who had heard the shot, Nampuh decided to save the stagecoach for another day and rejoin his renegade companions.

****

Paiute Joe came over the ridge and entered the south end of the valley along Reynolds Creek. He walked the game trail on the west side of the valley. By the light of a full moon he could see the stage road and the few scattered homesteads in the valley. He walked quietly over the trail, shifting the Enfield rifle to his left hand for better balance. Slung over his shoulder were the leather cartridge box and leather cap box. Against the chill, he wore a dark blue Union Army coat over his buckskin clothes. The coat had been a gift from the Commander at Camp Lyon for agreeing to be their tracker.

When Paiute Joe left Camp Lyon the previous day, soldiers were heading up Cow Creek to log pine trees for their protected quarters. A small number of soldiers remained at the campsite to shape the logs and begin assembling the dwellings. He understood there would be more soldiers coming to live at the camp. His assignment was to travel down Reynolds Creek to the Snake River and return to Camp Lyon. He was to report back to the Commander any signs of either Whites or Indians who were preying on travelers and settlers.

How the White man could divide the land with an invisible line puzzled Paiute Joe. The Commander talked of the Oregon Territory being west of camp and the Idaho Territory being east of camp. The land had always just been there for his people to use, with no invisible lines.

As he walked, melancholy crept into his heart. He thought of how his small Tago band of Paiutes had lived in this region since the beginning of time. His father had been Captain of their small band living within the Owyhee Mountains. Now all were dead, except his brother and wife. He and his brother had shared the woman and shared their son, but their band did not grow. They hunted game together and each year went to the Snake River to fish salmon and hunt birds. Over time it became harder to find other Paiutes to trade with and conduct joint hunts with. The time came when his brother wanted to live further in the high desert, away from the Whites. Paiute Joe decided to stay where he had been born. It was a sad time. Now, the Paiutes were dying of starvation or being killed by the Whites for trying to feed themselves. How it all had changed.

Memories of how they worked and lived together flooded Paiute Joe. He had enjoyed watching their wife pick currants and huckleberries. He had felt great pleasure at working with the family during the spring and summer to prepare food for the cache pits or caves. He recalled the full, rich smells that accompanied this work: roasted game was dried and pounded for storage, mixed with the aroma of chokecherry cakes drying in the sun. His favorite food was pounded meat mixed with blood and fat. They would laugh and talk at the meals. It satisfied his soul. Each spring they would start the process all over again. He still carried the obsidian knife with a juniper handle used by his family for preparing food.

Paiute Joe thought of his Grandfather and a pang of grief hit his stomach. He missed his wisdom and kindness. He thought of Grandfather smiling, with his white hair and wrinkled parchment skin. He was unsure at times if this mind view of Grandfather was imagination or a touch of his spirit. As a boy, Paiute Joe spent more time with Grandfather than anyone else in his family. He would listen spellbound to each of Grandfather's stories. Sometimes Grandfather would repeat a story many times, but Paiute Joe never mentioned this, out of respect for Grandfather and respect for the story.

He could see Grandfather animated, acting out stories. The coyote, Grandfather's favorite story animal, captured Paiute Joe's imagination. He loved tales of trickery and of how the coyote helped his people survive. The coyote used magic to change his form, becoming a swift antelope or noble hawk. Moral teachings came with each story, emphasizing the high value of courage and honesty, and how these virtues helped his people prosper. With a deep serious voice, Grandfather would warn that coyote magic could have a destructive impact on the family, if misused.

Grandfather taught him the ways of animals. Paiute Joe remembered his first kill. He had practiced endlessly with the adladl to perfect how he launched the flint-tipped arrow.

A young antelope buck in the brush stood motionless, blending in with the fall colors of the mountain mahogany. He saw two small spikes protruding from the top, and its quivering body. He raised the adladl and sent the arrow straight to the antelope's heart. The animal took one leap straight up and fell to the ground dead. Grandfather was very proud of him and gave much praise over the clean kill. The meat would be used to feed the whole band. The young antelope's soul was honored with the proper song and dance.

Paiute Joe became humble when he thought of his Grandfather's ocean of patience with him. Grandfather guided him through the world and taught how all things have a soul. All life, whether animal or plant, was respected, and each season was welcomed with rituals.

Where Grandfather touched Paiute Joe the most was in the development of his spirit. Patiently, Grandfather instructed him in the Sacred Silence. He taught him how to be passive and to silence his mind. With the mind silenced, the thoughts could be pure and clear as the mountain stream. From the pure mind, Paiute Joe was led to use imagination and bridge the gap between the flesh and the spirit. Grandfather taught how to read the signs and symbols of the spirit world, how to interpret his dreams and be guided by the Creator.

Most troubling for Paiute Joe were the dreams at first. Without his Grandfather's guidance he would never have found peace. Grandfather asked him about his dreams, and what they might mean. He told Grandfather of a recurring dream in which two hawks would attack each other. First they would fight in the air, then land on the ground and continue the struggle. Many times Paiute Joe would awake from a dream of hawks locked in a death-dance. This dream had started when he was a boy and continued as he grew older. In the last dream, the hawks had fought in the air and had again landed on the ground to continue the fight, but this time they just stared at each other and did not attack. They flew away.

Paiute Joe's Grandfather asked, "What is the meaning of this dream?"

"I am unsure, Grandfather."

In a quiet, soft voice the Grandfather asked, "What does your soul say? Listen carefully."

The young man paused and then replied, "I believe it means that I am to be a man of peace for both the Indian and the White man."

The Grandfather nodded his head in agreement. He said, "Be mindful of the coyote and watch for his leading."

When his Grandfather died, it was left to Paiute Joe to prepare the body and conduct the ritual that would take him to the afterlife. He fought back his tears and sadness in order to perform the proper rituals for his deceased Grandfather. The body was painted with markings of honor and a sad dirge was sung. The family placed grandfather's body within a cave, never to return there again.

Emerging from his memories to the awareness of the trail, the tracker felt a gentle breeze on the back of his neck. Shapes in the valley and on the mountains were becoming distinct. Paiute Joe changed course from the valley edge toward the center of the valley and the canyon entrance. He could see a sandstone ridge at the far end of the valley.

Suddenly the early morning silence was ruptured by the blast from a rifle. He knew the sound of this kind of rifle - the kind commonly used by Indians. The shot came from close to the canyon entrance. Paiute

Joe stopped and listened. He heard the far-off whinny of a horse, and headed toward the shot.

In the morning light, Paiute Joe looked over the ridge and down on the creek. Two hundred yards away on the other side of the creek, among the spring grass and sagebrush, he saw a body lying on the ground. He scanned the surrounding mountains for danger. All there was, was the smell of dust and moisture in the air, the early summer weather in the mountains, green, with random patches of sunflowers.

Paiute Joe heard a low rumble. He looked behind him and saw the stagecoach coming down the valley. Four matching black horses pulled the mudwagon, two men sitting atop. The canvas side-covers looked white against the dark wood of the stage and a cloud of dust billowed from behind. From the creek bank a lone coyote dashed from cover and headed downstream toward the high walls of the canyon entrance.

The stage passed and was half way up the steep grade before Paiute Joe moved from his cover. He stepped into the open sunlight and moved cautiously toward the campsite. When he reached the creek and willows, he found what he expected - the moccasin prints of Indians, one set of prints, huge in size, belonging to Nampuh. He and his band had been responsible for many vicious murders. Indians and Whites alike feared Nampuh.

Paiute Joe came up on a young man lying in his bedroll face up. He could see the blood on his shirt and a hole from the bullet entry. The young man looked dead. Pauite Joe squatted down close to him and looked more closely. He placed his hand to the partially opened mouth. He thought he felt breath. Next, he laid his hand on the young man's heart and felt it beat faintly.

Paiute Joe rose, tightened his headband, and moved his long black hair to one side. He squatted down and moved the bedroll cover aside. He lifted the young man and put him over his broad shoulder, then shifted the weight for balance. The square, dark face of Paiute Joe showed the strain of the man's weight. He began walking toward the canyon entrance. Paiute Joe would take him to his cave, where he stored his winter cache of food and supplies.

TWO

Paiute Joe laid the young man down by the entrance to the cave. He removed several tightly fit stones from the worn lava entrance. The doorway was small and Paiute Joe needed to crouch down to enter. He reached back and dragged the wounded man through, into a cave, located in a sheer section of the canyon above the scree line. Inside was a large dome shaped room that could easily accommodate six people. A hole in the ceiling permitted light to enter from the outside. It was not a direct chimney to the outside, but an angular shaft that permitted smoke to exit and light to be reflected through it.

The wall at the back of the cave was darker. Water seeped down into a natural bowl in the floor of the cave. From there a carved trench ran along the wall and looked to exit the cave entrance. Fresh, clear water was available in the cistern at all times.

The sidewall had a ledge and recess that went back several feet. Within this space were stored the supplies to survive the winter. All the clothing, cooking implements and processed food were kept here - high and dry - within leather storage bags, clay pots, and woven sage baskets.

From the storage ledge, Paiute Joe took a rabbit fur blanket and a trade blanket. He spread out the fur blanket, placed Jacob Deary on it, and removed his clothes. Around the neck of the young man was a leather necklace with a gold key on it. Paiute Joe lifted the key into his hand and noticed that the shaft had been bent, probably from being struck by the bullet. He removed the necklace and placed it on top of the pile of clothes to the side of the cave entrance.

Paiute Joe went to the pool of water and filled a clay bowl. He took a piece of antelope leather and dipped it into the bowl of water till it was soft and supple, then cleaned the angry, red wound of the White man. The White man looked deathly pale. The Indian watched his chest rise and fall with each shallow breath.

A black beetle awkwardly walked along the floor of the cave. It came to the arm of the wounded man and began to crawl up. It fell back, tried to climb the arm again and fell back. The third time it started up the arm it found purchase and went up and over the arm and onto the abdomen of the young man. Paiute Joe watched a moment and then put the back of his hand on course with the beetle. It crossed the youth's stomach and stepped on the waiting hand. Paiute Joe moved his hand to the ground and the beetle walked off and continued his journey across the cave floor. The Indian then placed the wool blanket over the man and pulled it to the bottom of his rib cage.

The Indian went back to the storage ledge and pulled out the wooden hearth-drill and bow string. With the hearth-drill came a leather pouch with sage and wood chips, used to start a fire. In the center of the cave, he began working the bowstring and blowing on the fine chips at the friction point. Smoke began to rise and a small flame appeared. He tipped the hearth, and the smoking, flaming chips fell into a larger pile of sage and wood in the fire pit. Leaving the fire to burn, he slung an empty storage pouch over his shoulder and exited the cave.

Three hours passed before he returned. He looked over at Jacob Deary. He was still breathing. His color had changed from ashen to a soft pink. The blanket was still as it had been placed on him, so he had not stirred. The smell of sage was strong in the cave. The fire had burned down, but not out. He placed more wood chips on the coals and blew on them until the flame grew.

From below the storage ledge, Paiute Joe picked up a worn bowl-shaped stone with one hand and with the other hand, a stone cylinder. He brought the mortar and pestle back to the center of the cave. From the pouch around his neck he withdrew the contents, and, squatting next to the stone bowl, placed into it purple coneflower blossoms and garlic roots.

At first the herbs were hard to grind, but slowly he worked them into a lavender paste. Paiute Joe went to the pool of water, dipped the clay bowl, filled it with water, and brought it back to his workspace. He dipped his fingers into the bowl, flicking drops of water into the working paste. He maintained his grinding action until he had enough medicine to fill the palm of his hand. Paiute Joe went to where Jacob lay and spread the medicine over the bullet wound. He could feel the dryness of the young man's skin. Next, he dipped a piece of rawhide into the bowl of water and let it soak up the water. He held the water-soaked antelope skin over Jacob's mouth, and then with the other hand pulled down on the jaw so that the lips parted. The other hand squeezed on the skin and the drops of cool water went into Jacob's mouth. Paiute

Joe continued to feed drops of water until the bowl was empty. He returned to the center of the cave, crossed his legs and began to meditate.

An hour later Paiute Joe repeated the making of the fresh herb poultice and the giving of the water. He sat back and entered the Sacred Silence until late that night. Finally, he was exhausted, curled up along the wall to sleep. He knew that the morning would tell whether the young man would live or die.

The Indian was awakened by the moans of the wounded man. Paiute Joe pushed himself into a sitting position and wiped the sleep from his eyes. Again he used the bow and wood chips to create a fire in the center of the cave. With the light from the fire, he could see the red from fever in Jacob's face. The moans were not from pain but from delirium. Paiute Joe placed his hand on the White man's forehead and grimaced with how hot it felt. He knew that if the fever were not broken the man would die.

Paiute Joe took the bowl, and dipped it in the cistern, and began to wash Jacob with cold water. He placed a cold, soaked skin across the forehead. Still the moans and unintelligible words came. Jacob Deary moved his head from side to side as though he were talking with someone. Paiute Joe chanted and prayed as he wiped the burning body with cold, wet skins. The Indian knew that the young man's fate would be determined soon.

****

It had just been blackness for Jacob Deary, then the heat started. It was relentless, engulfing. From its heart came a slow delirium that blossomed into madness.

"Where's the gold, Jake? I thought you left here to get the gold. Where's the gold?"

From a soft white fog came Jacob's friend Benjamin Helm.

"Jacob, we're counting on you to make us rich."

Then Benjamin's father appeared.

"Reverend Helm, why are you here? What's going on?" Jacob asked.

Reverend Helm slowly walked over to his son and put his hand on Benjamin's shoulder and spoke, "Why? We are here to do God's work and to make sure you find the gold." With his other hand he reached down and behind and retrieved a bucket. The Reverend held out a blue bucket brimming with gold nuggets. Nuggets were spilling over the side and onto the ground. Jacob wondered how the man could hold that heavy bucket straight out so easily. It all looked so odd.

"We told you what to look for and where, Jacob. Why haven't you found the gold?"

"I am looking. I will leave right now to go look for the gold."

Looks of disbelief appeared on the phantom faces.

"Believe me, I will find the gold. I will find it."

The two old friends from Oregon faded into the fog. Jacob struggled to get going on his quest for gold. His legs felt heavy as lead and his will was frustrated.

Out of the fog came two more people - Jacob's Mother and Father. They stood side by side looking at their son with affection.

"Father, Mother, I thought you were dead." Feelings of love rose in Jacob's heart. He could almost touch his parents.

His Father Philip spoke first. "Where is your brother, Basil?"

"He's with the woman who took care of Mom before she died. Don't you remember?" Feelings of frustration began to rise.

Again the Father spoke. "Where is your sister, Edna?"

"She's with Reverend Dickenson. Remember, Father? I stayed with Towner Savage after you died."

"Why did you let your brother and sister leave?"

"How could I take care of them, Father? I had no money, please understand, they were babies."

Guilt and frustration mixed together, tightening like ropes around Jacob's chest.

His Mother spoke. "Jacob, you stole the key to my jewel box."

"Yes, I did. I had to, Mother, don't you understand?"

"To steal from your Mother? We did not raise you to do such things."

"I have the gold key and will not return it. It was under your pillow for me to take."

"We came to take you with us, Jacob, but not if you are a thief."

"You are dead, Mother, it is the only thing I have to remember you by."

The Father and Mother slowly began to fade into the gray mist.

"Mother, Father please don't leave. Why are you leaving? I love you, please stay and talk with me."

They faded into the gray and Jacob returned to the blackness and fever. It was like being in hell. He tossed, calling out again for his Mother and Father. It was a nightmare of guilt and frustration.

****

Paiute Joe lay sleeping on the floor of the cave. It was early in the morning, hours before the sun would come up. The calls and motion of the sick man awakened him. The Indian felt his forehead and his heart sank. The fever was worse. The young man would die unless it was brought down. Again Paiute Joe used the bow to start a fire.

Paiute Joe dipped skins into the cold water and placed them on the dying man. He inspected the wound. The poultice was still in place and the area where the bullet had entered had not swollen. The Indian knew he must look further for the source of heat. He reached over and slowly turned Jacob onto his side. The young man made a low groan of protest, but remained unconscious. The Indian reached to the back opposite where the bullet entered and found the skin below the shoulder blade hot and hard. Again the Indian pressed against the skin. The infection had made the skin tight and hot. He pressed harder, finding a lump just under the skin. He pressed again and Jacob winced. He knew the hard knot was the bullet.

For the young man to have any chance to live, it would need to be removed. Paiute Joe took a deep breath and reached for his obsidian knife and the bowl of water and skin towels. The Indian held the juniper handle, laid the blade against the taut skin, drawing it in a straight line just above the hard spot under the skin. Immediately, the skin opened and from it poured hard, white chunks of pus, flowing down Jacob's back. Paiute Joe pressed on the sides of the flesh to try to push out the bullet. It remained lodged in the flesh and the Indian had to pull it out with his fingers. From behind it flowed still more infected mater, then blood, then finally clear liquid came from the wound. The Indian left the wound flowing, to stop on its own.

He prepared a new poultice for the wound, laying Jacob on his stomach to let the poultice harden. He noticed that the drainage had changed to water and that the putrefied poison had stopped flowing. He scooped up the reworked purple coneflower and garlic poultice into his hand and smeared it over the incision. The young man lay on his stomach with his head turned toward Paiute Joe. The Indian looked into the young man's face. The torture and grief were gone. When the poultice hardened, the Indian turned the White man onto his back.

Now, the Indian stopped long enough to appraise the situation. For the first time he noticed a stench of death in the cave. The infected flesh and smoke had mingled to create a repulsive smell. He resolved to clean the cave. He had done all that could be done for the young man. He would either heal or the Indian would find a suitable burial place for him. Paiute Joe felt contented in his soul.

With the first light he began to clean the cave. All the infected skins and utensils were taken to the stream and washed. He built a larger fire to kill the smell in the cave. He would look for fresh food outside rather than relying on the cache of food. Paiute Joe packed up and prepared to leave. He left a strong fire and slipped out the cave entrance.

****

Jacob Deary felt the exhalation of his breath and the pain in his shoulder at the same time. Again the incoming air, exhalation, and pain.

"Was this a dream? Where is the heat?" he thought. He woke in confusion about where he was, and just what had happened to him. The confusion swam in his head and then he opened his eyes. Light from the fire danced on the walls of the cave and a small dark blue opening could be seen at the top of the ceiling. Then the putrid smell of death hit his nostrils and the cave began to move. Next, Jacob found himself half-turned and puking bile out of his stomach. The strain of the heaves pulled his damaged muscles and sent waves of pain through his body. He collapsed back into unconsciousness.

Paiute Joe returned to the cave with six quail, cleaned and readied for cooking, and some camas roots. He stoked the fire and began cooking. He could see that the young man had stirred. He reached over and put his hand against his forehead. The hard heat of fever was gone. The young man felt hot, but not the brutal heat just before death. For the first time Paiute Joe felt that the young man would live. The Indian noticed yellow bile from where he had thrown up and knew that he had regained consciousness.

The Indian boiled the camas plants and slowly turned the quail - two at a time - over the fire with willow sticks run through them. When they finished cooling he handpicked the meat off them and placed it in a bowl. In another bowl he cut up the camas into small bits. The camas would be easy to scoop up and eat with his hands. The Indian restoked the fire, putting the two bowls of food and a bowl of fresh water close to the wounded man. Paiute Joe again left the cave to hunt.

It was late afternoon before Jacob Deary regained consciousness. The cave was lighter, from the fire, from the opening above and from the entrance. Jacob could see the Indian trappings and a sharp jab of adrenaline pumped into his system from fear. But it didn't make sense. If he was in danger then why was he alive and in a protected cave? Or was this his cage?

He brought himself up on his left elbow and looked about him. The three bowls were in view and the scent of cooked meat brought saliva to his mouth. Jacob edged up into a sitting position, doing his best to protect his wounded right chest. Any movement brought pain, but his desire for fresh water and food drove him past the pain. He lifted the bowl of water and drank in large satisfying gulps. Excess water spilled out the edge and down his chest. Its sharp cold felt refreshing to the skin. He drank the entire bowl of water and then began to eat the cooked quail. The pieces of meat contained no bone, making it easy to pick them up to eat. Jacob was aware of the care that was taken to prepare this food. He ate until the meat was gone. He lifted the third bowl with the camas plant, and scooped its sweet contents into his mouth.

This was the first food eaten in many days. He sat leaning against his locked good arm, sated with food and water, and only sleep possessed him. Leaning back down onto the blanket, he pulled the rabbit skin blanket over him and fell into a deep sleep.

The following morning Jacob Deary awoke. He had the deep groggy feeling of a long night. The fever was gone. However, there was a sharp pain in his right shoulder. He woke with the need to relieve himself. He thought, "How long has it been?" The need to urinate pushed him into a sitting position and he felt a movement in his bowels. Jacob saw an empty bowl placed at the far end of the cave, and dragged himself to it. With one hand he braced himself against the cave wall and relieved himself. The strain brought sweat to his forehead and he felt faint. He fought to stay conscious, got the job done, and was relieved that all was working. He placed the refuse bowl close to the entrance and looked about the cave.

He saw a cistern of water in the far corner and edged himself over to it, while protecting his wounded shoulder. He put his finger into the water to feel its temperature, and then leaned close over its reflective surface to examine his face. A lock of golden brown hair that had been matted to his head from sweat and dirt fell into the water. He raised up, brushed his hair back with his hand, and again leaned over the water to see himself. The sight that reflected back startled him. The unshaven, sunken-cheeked face was his, but looked much older and sicker. Jacob dipped a small bowl into the water and drank it in large satisfying gulps. When he finished, he returned to his sleeping area and gave in to his fatigue. Again he fell into a deep healing sleep.

It was late afternoon before Paiute Joe returned to the cave. He smelled the stench of waste and sweat. He began a fire with the drill, placing pieces of sage onto it to purify the air. He left with the bowls to clean them, and returned to prepare food for the injured man. Again the Indian prepared quail, picking the meat free of bones, and placing it in a bowl. He boiled camas plants and placed them along side the quail meat. This time Paiute Joe ate his own meal in the cave. The Indian knew it would not be long before the young man was strong enough to leave, maybe as soon as tomorrow.

The shadows from the low flames of the fire danced against the cave walls. Paiute Joe remembered the happy times his family had spent here. He felt sadness as he thought of his brother and wife and son. He missed their love and company. Late at night is when these thoughts bothered him. The Indian patiently waited for the young man to wake.

Paiute Joe was placing more wood onto the fire when Jacob moved, turned his head toward the fire, and opened his eyes. Jacob Deary looked directly at the Indian. Then he began the painful task of raising up on one arm to be upright.

Once in the sitting position Jacob asked, "How long have I been here?"

The Indian replied, "Seven days."

The Indian sat with crossed legs opposite the White man.

Time was a blur, part dream and part nightmare. His throat was dry. The Indian sensed his need for water and passed the young man a full bowl. Jacob eagerly drank it all and looked back at the Indian. His tobacco-colored skin showed age. The older man radiated a mood of serenity.

Jacob asked, "Who shot me?"

Paiute Joe replied, "Nampuh".

It still did not make sense to Jacob, but somehow he knew it was another Indian and the memories were a whirl in his mind. He just was not able to make sense of it all.

"You brought me here?"

"Yes."

The Indian passed the bowl of quail meat to Jacob and he eagerly accepted. He began scooping the meat into his mouth. When he finished he gave the empty bowl back to the Indian.

"You saved my life."

"The Creator spared your life."

"Thank you for your help."

Paiute Joe acknowledged the young man with a nod of the head.

"You will be well enough to travel by tomorrow. I will be gone before morning. Dried food will be here for you when you wake. I wish you well. Place the stones in front of the cave entrance."

Jacob thought it amusing that the Indian was telling him to close the door when he left.

"I will."

Jacob woke and was chilled and sore. The fire had burned down to warm embers and the pain and soreness were almost overpowering. He did notice that the swelling had gone down slightly. He sat up and looked around the cave. It had been cleaned, and close to where Jacob lay were his pants and a shirt belonging to the Indian. He reached over and pulled the buckskin shirt over his head, awkwardly pushing his arm through the armhole. He slid his old pants on while still sitting. Sweat formed on his forehead from the effort.

Jacob saw the last of his possessions - the gold key he stole from under his mother's pillow. He lifted the leather lace it was tied to and held it up to look at. He could see where the bullet had bent the shaft. Jacob started to place the leather necklace over his head and stopped. He looked at the gold key and then placed it with the leather lace into the wooden bowl beside his bed.

"Maybe the Indian can make good use of this."

THREE

"You lop-eared mutt, stop!" Little Mac spoke harshly, protecting his face with his shoulder, and trying to get back to tightening the crotch chain, as he lay under his freight wagon.

The dog backed up and tilted its head, waiting for another opening. It came. Rat moved forward quickly, sticking its cold nose against Little Mac's cheek, and with one motion, applying a long, wet draw of the tongue up the side of its owner's face.

"Stop." He brushed the dog away and completed tightening the chain.

The spotted squat dog backed up, satisfied that it had hit its target. One ear pointed straight up and the other bent over and pointed down. Its short wiry hair was stiff and hard to the touch. Little Mac and Rat were a team. They had found each other down by the Snake River, and Rat had tagged along with him ever since. Rat was no beauty and Little Mac was no kid. Rat was smart. Little Mac saw value in the dog when it began to help the mules cross the jerk-line. It never spooked them; it gave just enough nip and bark to encourage them to cross over.

The freighter had come from the Democrats, the last stage station before the hard pull over the mountain. He had left the lead wagon there and had taken his trail wagon to the top of the mountain, returning to the station on Reynolds Creek with the mules to spend the night. Early the following morning, he brought up the lead wagon, coupled the two together, and was readying for the sharp descent into Booneville. This trip was different from other freight trips; his sidekick had abandoned him at Brunzell's Hotel further back. Booze and women had lured the swamper, and when morning came he had been nowhere to be found.

Little Mac knew he'd have his hands full for the trip down the mountain. Even for two men it was work, but alone it could be dangerous, although the two Schuttler wagons tracked well and were easy to pull. He slid out from under, brushed himself off, and stood next to the larger lead wagon. Little Mac was six feet tall and the sides of the wagons were taller. The rear wagon wheels were larger in diameter than the front wheels. The second wagon was a little smaller, with a lower load capacity. Little Mac stood back, furled his brow, and considered the problems of making the steep descent into Booneville without help. The wagons were sturdy and not overloaded. They were packed full, the load tied down to the sideboards - clothing and dry goods, an average load.

The freighter went to the jockey-box and took his gloves out, pulled them tight on his hands, looked at the five mule teams and considered their safety. Eight mules, all seasoned veterans of this trail. However, with freighting anything could happen. Next, he rechecked the wagons. Prior to this trip, all the wheels had been removed, and the hub bands tightened by lapping linseed oil-soaked canvas over the hub, and driving the bands tight with the spokes. Little Mac doubted there would be any trouble from the wheels.

From the shoe hook on the stringer, he removed one brake shoe. Going to the lead wagon he removed a second one. He attached the shoe and collar to one rear wheel of each wagon. This would keep the back wheel from turning, and the wagons from picking up too much speed going downhill. A rough lock chain connected the brake shoe and iron half circle under the front axle of each wagon.

The wagons were ready to move out, the mules getting restless and moving from side to side. This morning's preparation had taken longer than normal. Another hand would have been welcome.

****

Jacob Deary could see the freighter was checking his wagons before starting out. Five teams of mules were standing in their harnesses waiting for the signal to move. Jacob caught his breath, adjusted the bedroll draped over his good shoulder and stood, light headed, until his breath came easily. It had been a two-day walk. The injury was still taking its toll.

From around the second wagon came the freighter with a tan canvas coat, and a worn, wide-brimmed hat. He was lean and moved with purpose. Standing off the road and close to the mountain rim was a stranger, a White man, in Indian clothes.

"Odd." Little Mac thought. As the man moved forward, Little Mac could see he was young, maybe in his teens or twenties, and that he was skinny and pale. Little Mac could see the outline of his cheekbones.

The young man approached. He said out loud and to himself, "God, another fortune hunter coming on a shank mare."

Close up, the young man spoke, "Mornin'."

"Mornin'." Little Mac replied.

At this distance, Little Mac could see that the stranger had an injured shoulder. A spot of blood stained the leather shirt. The young man spoke again.

"I could use a ride, maybe trade you for some work."

"Lad, you look a bit sickly to do much work, and you're protecting that right arm."

"I will do the work."

Rat walked out from under one of the teams. The dog tilted its head and looked at Jacob. Little Mac thought it unusual that the dog did not bark.

Little Mac rubbed his chin, thinking of the possibilities.

"Well, I could use a swamper, that is, if you are willin'?"

"Sure." Jake replied. He stuck out his left hand to shake Little Mac's.

"I'm Jacob Deary."

"Little Mac, lad. This is Rat." - tilting his head toward the dog. "Well, Jacob, what I need you to do - at least on this steep descent - is to walk on down the road 'till you can't hear the ham bells. I'll be making some noise for a bit and then I'll start down the grade and pick you up. How's that sound? You can ride the rest of the way to Booneville with me. When you get to where you can't hear my bells, you listen real hard for any ham bells coming the other way. If you hear bells, you yell like hell. We don't want two rigs meeting on this road. I have paid the $10.00 toll for this road and don't want to lose my money and my rigs. When I pick you up down below, you can steady the brake."

Jacob nodded in agreement, walked over to the lead wagon and tossed his bedroll under the seat. He turned and began walking down the road.

Little Mac went to the leaders and tugged on the ham bells. The bells rang, the sound carrying on the cool morning air. Little Mac continued to ring the ham bells intermittently. He paused, pulled out his pocket watch and thought, "Fifteen more minutes, and I will start out."

Little Mac put his watch away, giving one more pull on the ham bells before starting down the mountain. He swung himself up on Mary, the near wheeler mule. Mary was as calm as always and easily accepted Little Mac onto her back. From the back of the mule Little Mac could reach the bullwhip if he needed to use it. He took the left jerk line in his left hand, the right jerk line in the other and paused to listen for a call from Jacob. All was quiet. He called out "Haw," and gave a tug with his left hand to turn the young lead mule. With shudder and jerk the two wagons moved forward and toward the left. Rat came up beside the second team of mules, alerting them to step briskly over the chain as they began the turn. The frozen rear wheels made a scraping sound as the wagons gained speed, and Little Mac felt secure with the familiar chuck. He kept his ears alert for a call or the sound of bells over the noise.

Jacob had moved quickly down the road. It had been easy going. He continued down the steep winding road, listening for the sound of ham bells ringing from below. Jacob could hear Little Mac ringing his ham bells at measured intervals. There was a long interval, then the rings started up again. Jacob decided to wait for the freighter on the bank beside the road.

He found a long straight stretch of road. Here would be a good place to stop the two-wagon freight outfit in an orderly fashion. The grade was not too steep and Little Mac would have an easy time slowing the wagons. Jacob leaned back against the bank and took a deep breath. His shoulder pain was not as sharp as before. Probably the drainage from the wound had slowed. He looked at the narrow road and reflected how the freighter kept the long unwieldy rigs from tumbling over at each turn. The road was full of ruts from travel, and the ruts were filled in with sugar dust. The ride was rougher than it looked.

From up the road Jacob heard ham bells. The leaders appeared round the bend. Rat was pushing the sixes over the chain, and sprinting back to the second team. The turn was sharp, and the lead team climbed up the bank to allow the following teams to round the bend, with the wagons trailing in the center of the road. The mules crossed back over the chain and came straight down the road toward Jacob.

Little Mac pulled back on the jerk line and yelled "Wow." He looked over to Jacob from the back of Mary and said, "Glad to see you aren't snooz'n'."

Jacob smiled and rose, brushed the dust from the back of his pants with his left hand and walked to the lead wagon.

Little Mac said, "I could use you to steady that brake lever. The road steep'ns up from here into town."

Jacob grabbed the sideboard with his left hand, swung himself halfway up, and then used the front wheel to climb onto the seat. He slid over to the off side and pulled the lever, placing it in the ratchet, which just barely put pressure on the wheel. Jacob knew the pressure could be increased when the wagons began moving down and the road became steep. The S iron rode high on the hub and extra pressure would be needed for braking.

Little Mac called to the mules and they began moving. Again the wagons jerked to a start and then settled into a steady rolling motion.

Jacob looked down at the S iron to see its placement on the wheel. By the motion of the wagons Jacob felt like they were under control. He looked over the side of the wagon and straight down the mountain into the ravine below. Despite the appearance of safety, from his perch on the wagon their position felt tentative. If the wagon went over the edge, it was all over.

They had traveled three miles before Jacob saw rooftops, smoke rising from the chimneys, and heard sounds from the town below. For the first time since being shot, feelings of anticipation and adventure returned. Jacob continued to apply even pressure to the brake lever with his left hand.

Little Mac turned his head sideways and asked, "You have any family here?"

"No, they're all dead. I have some brothers and sisters that other families took back in Oregon."

"How old are ya, lad?"

"Nineteen."

"You ever been in this country before?"

"I came through the Snake River Valley with my family, when we came West with the wagon train."

"These Owyhees are tough country. This first town down below is Booneville."

"Up the creek a ways is a newer town called Ruby City. It's the county seat. Further up the creek is Silver City. They are finding rich paydirt up toward Silver City and people are building up the area. High pay dirt for silver and gold all the way up this canyon."

"Well, I came here to make money."

"If you don't mind me ask'n', where'd ya get the Injun clothes?"

"I was shot and robbed by Nampuh and an Indian nursed me back to health. He gave me some of his clothes."

"You are mighty lucky, lad. I'm unloading in Ruby City and putting my stock up with Hill Beachy for a day. There's a hotel - The Idaho Hotel - on the West Side of Main Street, ya can't miss it. Go to the back and ask for Hosea Eastman. He and his sister-in-law run the hotel. You tell him that Little Mac said to give you a job. They are always looking for kitchen help. Maybe you can get your health back and strike it rich. Remember, you strike it rich, ya owe me a drink."

"Thanks."

The freight outfit came to the short straight stretch before crossing the creek into Booneville. The road was narrow and homes and buildings were sandwiched in tightly. Dogs came out from under and behind every building and greeted the freight outfit, barking and yelping. The veteran mules paid little attention and allowed Rat to return bark for bark. The mules made the sharp turn onto the main road. Little Mac stopped the freight outfit and removed the brake shoes. Jacob climbed off the seat, helping as best he could with the chain and shoes. He put the brake lever back into the neutral position and took in the scenery.

Up the mountainsides he could see the tailing piles and holes made by the miners. In the creek men were panning, shoveling ore from the hillside into their sluice boxes. Everywhere was the sound of metal being worked in the blacksmith shop, hammers pounding nails, wagons hauling materials of all kinds, and people walking with purpose in every direction.

The freight outfit continued on a short distance to Ruby City. A haze of smoke filled the narrow valley in the late afternoon. The air was still, the sky was clear, and the air warm. Where the road flattened out on the left was a gentle slope where older homes and businesses were mingled with new construction. Streets were laid out in orderly fashion. Jacob sighted a stable and corral partially hidden behind some buildings. The road ahead branched into a "Y". Little Mac brought the outfit to a halt and pointed up the street.

"See that white two-story building?"

"Yes."

"That's the best hotel in Ruby City." Little Mac reached into his breast pocket and pulled out a five-dollar gold piece and turned back to Jacob.

"Here, take this. Ya earned it."

Jacob paused, then reached down and took the gold. He needed the money. He slipped it into his britches pocket and climbed off the lead wagon. Grabbing his bedroll he turned to Little Mac, and said with gratitude in his voice, "Thanks. Hope I meet up with you again."

"You will, lad. Take care." Little Mac turned back, hollering "Gee" for the freight outfit to get moving.

Jacob walked toward the hotel and looked over the people going in and out. Some of the men were dressed well, but most were in work clothes. Jacob noticed two of the men with women who probably were their wives. As he got closer to the hotel he looked for a path to the back where he might find Hosea Eastman.

Jacob found the back door and knocked. While he stood waiting for an answer he looked around. Two large storage sheds stood in the rear of the hotel. One had a closed door on it and the other was doorless, and filled with wood. More wood was stacked along the outside wall. A chopping block stood near by. There were wood chips scattered on the ground and an ax stuck in the block.

The back door to the hotel opened and a short, slight man with a handlebar mustache and bald head opened the door.

The man said, "Yes?"

"Little Mac said I could get work here. Are you Hosea Eastman?"

The owner took a long pause, looked the young man up and down, then shook his head yes, and stepped out the door, walking toward the sheds. Little Mac would not steer him wrong.

"Come. You clean the ash from the stoves, chop the wood and haul the water when needed. Understand? Don't over-stoke the stoves. The last man who had your job almost burned the place down last April." He said this while walking to the shed with a door, not looking at Jake. He reached the shed, opened the door and turned to Jacob.

"You stay here, eat two meals, and I pay you a dollar a day."

Looking past the open door, Jacob could see a sleeping cot and dresser.

"You be at the back door five in the morning. Understand?"

"Yes, sir."

****

Late in the day, Enoch Fruit hitched the twin bays to the buckboard and rode away from Fort Boise toward the Owyhee River. He was on the opposite side of the river from the fort, and out of direct observation by the Union soldiers. Soldiers and Indians alike knew Enoch. The law had a grudging acceptance of Enoch Fruit, since they never were able to catch him in illegal trading. Residents in the area had learned to tolerate him. Today he was headed up the Owyhee River with a load of trade items for Indians, covered with a blanket in the back of the buckboard. He continued up the river and around two bends before he stopped the horses and made a camp.

In the dark, the fire crackled and hissed from the wet wood. Enoch stroked his full beard and took another swallow of whiskey from the tin cup. He had a glow on, and he picked a stick from the side of the fire and poked at it, sitting cross-legged on the ground, his soiled hat pulled tightly on his head. He laughed out loud. The whiskey had him and it twisted his thoughts and imagination.

Enoch thought of his friend John Wheeler. He had not been seen for over a month. Last time the stage to Boise was robbed, John disappeared. Enoch figured John was behind the occasional stage robberies in the Snake River country. In the past, he and John had worked together trapping up by Farewell Bend. Times changed, people moved in, and the scarcity of the game made the two look for other ways to make money. Enoch still dressed like a trapper, wearing buckskin pants and Indian boots. He smelled terrible. When he smiled, the blackened rotting teeth showed a perfect match for the character within.

From the willows at the riverside of his camp emerged three figures. Enoch felt relieved the Indians were here. Nampuh' form loomed larger than the others' did. Their faces became distinct as they came into the glow of the firelight. Nampuh and the two braves now stood over Enoch as he sat by the fire sipping his whiskey. Enoch spoke first.

"About time you savages showed up." Enoch tilted his head to look at the trio and smiled, showing his rotten teeth and laughing softly.

Nampuh spoke, "You have the whiskey?"

Enoch replied, "You have the money?"

"As always." Loathing for Enoch showed in the huge Indian's face.

Nampuh sat on the ground and reached over, while Enoch reached behind, pulled out a bottle and handed it to the Indian. Nampuh put it to his mouth, tipped it up and drank all the contents. When he put the bottle down, anger and disgust had gone from his face and in their place was a relaxed satisfied look.

Few people knew that Nampuh spoke English, or that he was only half Indian. His mulatto features were more evident by the light of the campfire. The huge man weighed three hundred pounds and was solid muscle. No horse could carry him, so he walked or ran wherever he went. He was powered by a savagery and cruelty arising from deep within. Nampuh had come to the Owhyees over ten years earlier on a wagon train. One woman who had spurned his love, and one man who shamed the half-Indian, half-black man, were the kindling and match for his killing rage.

The two braves with Nampuh returned with a satchel and items wrapped, in a blanket, to be traded for whiskey. One of them leaned down and placed the satchel at Nampuh's knee. The other held the blanket-wrapped items. Enoch smiled at Nampuh. This is what he came for - gold and guns.

From a pack, Nampuh took two small leather pouches filled with gold dust and flung them to Enoch, who easily fielded the toss.

"How many cases of whiskey?" Nampuh asked.

"Four."

Enoch opened each pouch and poured out a bit of gold dust from each into his hand. "This will buy you three cases of whiskey, not four."

Nampuh motioned to one of the braves who brought up a blanket - wrapped bundle, set it on the ground, and undid the twine. Inside were two rifles, one of them a Springfield rifle. Enoch picked it up and inspected it. He showed no feeling.

"Done. Four cases of whiskey." Enoch rolled his head to one side and gave Nampuh a sideways grin.

"Someday I will take your scalp and wear it on my belt."

"As long as I bring the whiskey, you won't touch me."

The two braves went over to the buckboard, took out the four cases of whiskey and packed them back into the dark and willows. Nampuh and Enoch stood by the fire. Enoch held up his bottle and offered the Indian a drink. Nampuh took it, drinking half of the

Silver City

whiskey, and handed it back to Enoch, then turned and disappeared into the night.

Enoch threw more logs on the fire. He staggered a bit from the whiskey and then sat down. Pouring another drink into his cup he thought what a high price his whiskey brought, and how unquestioningly, the Indians paid it. The night wore on and Enoch passed out. He would return to Fort Boise when he came to in the morning.

****

Jacob woke at 4:45. He opened his eyes, sat on the edge of the narrow bed, rotating his shoulder till the stiffness eased, then went to a bowl of water and washed. The little stove was still hot from the night's stoking, and he poured hot water from a kettle into another bowl for shaving. The straight edge razor cut his day-old growth with ease. He dressed and then tied the tarboosh around his hair. Jacob found it easier to wear than a hat while he worked in the kitchen.

He knew his routine. He arrived at 5:00 to clean the cinder boxes on the two wood stoves. He next brought in some wood to fire the stoves, and stacked reserve wood on a small porch in the back. He would eat breakfast and then begin sawing and chopping the logs, which were brought in. When he finished the morning chores, he would return to the kitchen for further work the owners Hosea and his sister-in-law Mercy would have for him.

Hosea had been generous with him. The first day Hosea sent him to a bathhouse to clean up and shave and buy some clothes. He specifically forbade him to wear any Indian clothes. Jacob was given a place to sleep out back. Over the last three months, food and work helped to heal his body and make him hard and strong. When he was chopping wood, Jacob would look over at the back window of the kitchen and find Anna, Mercy's helper, looking out at him. When she saw him looking back, she would quickly turn away.

Jacob walked to the back of the hotel and into the kitchen. He pulled the metal boxes out from the Step-Top style cook stove. He carried the ash carefully to a pit behind the wood shed. Regardless of how carefully he cleaned the ash boxes, he invariably got ash on his face. He returned the ash boxes to the stove and loaded more wood in the firebox. A small stack of wood remained by the far wall from the previous day. He blew on the embers, raising the flame until the stove came alive. Jacob closed the firebox door. Next, he went into the dining area, stoked the parlor stove, and went to the turtle ash box. He put his foot on the turtle's head and the shell popped open, exposing the ash container. This container was also emptied in the pit, then used it to haul more wood into the hotel for heat and cooking.

"Jacob, come to breakfast." Mercy called.

He stopped his wood splitting and returned to the kitchen.

As Jacob came in the back door, the kitchen seemed alive with smells and activity - Mercy and Anna were at work preparing breakfast for the guests, the tea kettle spitting out its plume of steam, and the coffee pot giving off its full aroma. The sadirons rested on a shelf close to the stove. Food sizzled and smelled appetizing. Jacob went to his little table in the back corner and Anna brought him a plate of eggs. She gave Jacob a soft pleasant smile.

Anna was full figured and healthy looking. Her brown hair parted in the middle and pulled back into a bun contrasting her pink cheeks and rounded features. She wore a long full skirt with an apron over the top. Jacob figured she was about his age.

From the guest dining room a man with a black suit and black wide-brimmed hat walked into the kitchen area. In his right hand he carried a cigar. Mercy and Anna became more animated.

"Mornin'."

"Morning, Mr. Moore."

"May I grab a cup of coffee?"

"Certainly, Mr. Moore." Mercy went to the cupboard and retrieved a cup, pouring a cup of coffee for the guest.

"Thanks." He took out a match, struck it against the stovetop, lit his cigar, and returned to the dining room.

"Who's that?" Jacob asked.

Mercy turned and answered Jacob. "That's Marion Moore. He is involved with the Hays and Ray Mine up above where they're building in Silver City. He might be one of the people trying to buy it and rename it the Ida Elmore. He is such a gentleman. Always polite and pays his bill each week, with no questions asked. All the guests and locals like the man."

Jacob thought to himself, "From the fuss, Mercy and Anna both liked him."

A newspaper had been left on the table after breakfast. Jacob read from the Ruby City Avalanche dated September 2, 1865. "Mr. John Kelly, the natural vocalist and violinist, and his pupil, the Indian Prodigy, have arrived in Ruby City and will give one of their entertainments at the Magnolia Saloon this evening." Jacob was intrigued and promised himself to be at the show that evening.

Hosea stood in the storeroom doorway and informed Jacob that more timber would be showing up today. It was early fall and more would be needed for the winter. The local woodcutters needed to go further and further out to find the wood, and each load of wood was becoming more expensive, from the way Hosea frowned.

"Let me know if you need a hand unloadin'."

"I will." Jacob replied. He finished his plate and returned to the work outside.

The woodshed held tools and one cord of wood. Three more were stacked along its sides. As he grabbed the bucksaw, Jacob remembered how slow and sore he was at first. He cut four-foot lengths of juniper or mahogany to a size which fit the two stoves. He could barely lift the sledgehammer to pound the wedge through the knotty wood.

Anna picked up Jacob's plates to be washed, pausing a moment to watch him return to his room behind the hotel. She began scheming how she could avoid going to church tomorrow. Church services were held in a friend's clabbered home. A real church had not been erected yet and maybe never would be, the way Silver City was booming. Less attention was paid to Ruby City all the time. She could feign sickness. She could spend over two hours unattended. Her cheeks began to flush as she planned.

Jacob left his room and walked around the hotel, up Main Street, and then down a side street toward the Magnolia Saloon. It was early, but to delay would mean not getting in. Jacob knew the miners and townspeople would crowd to see the famous John Kelly and his adopted son. The Magnolia Saloon was the largest structure in Ruby City. Normally, the saloon catered to lonely miners who came to dance with the Hurdy Gurdy women. The bar charged a nice sum for a dance and would give the women under contract a small percent of the money. Occasionally, one of the women would find a man to marry and the man would buy out her contract from the bar.

Jacob opened the door and walked into the large expanse of the bar. In the far corner a makeshift stage had been erected for the performers. Jacob went to the bar, paid for his ticket, and ordered a drink of whiskey. The room was already half full of miners and townspeople. The atmosphere was charged with anticipation and good cheer. Extra chairs had been brought in, but the patrons were mostly standing. Jacob decided to go to the sidewall and stake out his vantage point. He leaned back against the wall and looked back over the crowd. Maybe it was the liquor, but he felt less pain in his shoulder and his spirits were the best since he was shot. It had taken three months for his wounds to heal.

He watched the barroom fill with people. The clock behind the bar was at ten minutes to seven. The noise level had increased, as alcohol and the multitude of people made for a loud, gay crowd. They were packed close together waiting for the performance to begin. At five minutes after seven a saloon worker with a white apron on came out onto the stage and placed oil lamps on its outer lip, lighting them. He went to the wall lamps and turned the wicks up, and the stage lit up brighter than the rest of the saloon. The worker squeezed his way through the crowd, and went to the remaining wall oil lamps, turning down their wicks. Now the stage area became the focus of attention. The double doors of the saloon entrance were open and people pressed together and gathered on the wooden walkway outside, to hear the performers. The worker left through a door at the end of the bar, which led to the back room. The crowd quieted.

From the side door came a portly man with a black bowler hat on. As he stepped onto the stage, the crowd roared, waving their hands in the air. The man went to a chair, which held his violin, picked it up and walked to the center of the stage, facing the crowd. The crowd continued to cheer. There stood John Kelly in his entire splendor. He looked at the crowd and gave them a half smile of appreciation. The Irishman had them all before he even lifted the violin to his chin. First he played a quick-tempoed piece, which had the crowd tapping their feet. As he played piece after piece, he varied the selections between songs of Ireland and frontier favorites. The music brought back memories of home, and of loves left behind.

John Kelly stopped playing for a moment and motioned toward the side door through which he had entered. The door opened, and from the dark opening stepped an Indian boy of about eight years old. It was difficult to see him until he stepped into the center of the stage. The boy, dressed in a suit, looked a bit out of place. John Kelly had adopted the boy after the Indian uprising on the Malheur River. Pride and love showed in the entertainer's face. Kelly had taught the boy to sing, dance and play the violin. The crowd welcomed him with a loud cheer, whistles, and clapping. John motioned to the people to be quiet, and the boy began playing the violin while John Kelly sang. All were spellbound.

The music carried throughout the town and went on till two in the morning. John Kelly and his Indian son were called back by the crowd two times. The miners and townspeople would not let them go. Finally, a few minutes after two, the last song ended and the stage was empty. The people began to leave and the oil lamps along the wall were turned up. Jacob looked at the faces of the audience and noticed streaks from tears on the faces of both men and women. Jacob had pushed away his memories of home and family. Tonight they were back in front of him and he missed his people terribly. He left the saloon and walked slowly back to his small room behind the hotel.

The next day was little different from any other Sunday morning. There was a dusting of snow on the ground and a light wind blowing up the canyon. Jacob completed his chores and returned to his room. He intended to laze the rest of the day. He lay back on the small bed, closed his eyes and began to drift off.

The door of the small shed was thrown open and closed quickly. Jacob, startled, opened his eyes. Light from the window dimmed his view and it took a few seconds for him to recognize the figure at the door.

"Anna?"

She did not say a word, but came to the side of the bed. Jacob read a purpose in her eyes.

"Shhh." She took the cuff of her dress sleeve and wiped the white ash from his forehead. She reached down and undid Jacob's pants and slid them down. Hoisting her skirt, she straddled Jacob and lowered herself down. She unbuttoned his shirt and ran her fingers over the scar of the bullet wound. Jacob rode the waves and did not say a word.

A lone coyote on the edge of town began howling.

FOUR

"Jake, you been here at the hotel going on two years. You've weathered two tough winters and haven't cut and run to the valley. You got a few dollars saved and the people around here think real well of you."

"Thanks, Mr. Moore. After I was shot, I wasn't sure life was ever going to be the same."

Marion Moore continued, "Since the Idaho Hotel moved up to Silver City and the new owners took over in Ruby City, this place hasn't been the same. I'm going to move up to Silver. I'll be closer to the mine and to friends. The new owners are alright, but it just isn't the same since the Eastmans moved. This place is going to die, and all the action will be up where the big mines are. Silver is the county seat now and that counts for a lot. I'm offering you work at the Ida Elmore Mine. We have officially got control of the Hays and Ray Mine, and some people from Portland are putting money into it to make it the richest mine in the West. We're always looking for good men."

"Well, I appreciate the offer, but I've been talking with Hill Beachy. He has the new stables in back of the Idaho Hotel in Silver City, and he's offered me work."

"You won't make the money working in a stable that you would looking for gold."

Silver City

"My original plans were to find all the gold up here. Now, working in a closed-in mine and chasing gold doesn't look as attractive. Maybe later on I would but right now my heart isn't in it. Mr. Beachy has reassembled the stables up at the hotel, and I've been helping him in my spare time. I want to get involved in livestock; in particular, horses - maybe sell them to the army or ship them back East."

"It takes money, lad, that's what I am try'n' to tell ya."

"You're right, but don't think I can do my time in the mine. Thanks anyway."

Marion Moore left the shed where Jake lived behind the hotel, walked around the side of the Ruby City hotel to the buckboard waiting out front. It was a short trip to Silver City. His possessions were loaded into the buckboard for the move to the new county seat.

Jacob knew his kitchen work was over and it was time to move on.

A week later he gave notice at the old Idaho Hotel, packed his bags, and caught a ride going to Silver City. He left the buckboard just after the bridge crosses Jordan Creek and began walking toward the new hotel. It was three stories high, long and large. He walked down Jordan Street, turned left just before the hotel and went behind to the stable. The winter snows were gone from the valley and only a smattering of snow remained on War Eagle and Florida Mountain.

Jacob thought the new hotel looked like a grand castle. Marion Moore was right about Silver City. It would overshadow the other mining towns below and become the center of activity from here on out. The street was alive with the sound of hammers, horses and riders going by, and freight wagons unloading their cargo. There were fewer dogs to harass the people and wagons. It looked cleaner and more civilized than Booneville or Ruby City. Houses in Ruby City were poorly built and looking dilapidated as soon as they were constructed. Silver City homes and business had more substance.

Life had changed again. He had hated to see Anna leave. She supplied the spice in life and she certainly could keep a secret. Anna needed a big city and Jacob wished her well.

Jacob went to the barn and walked through the open door. A stagecoach rested quietly at the back of the barn. A half dozen stalls were along the left side. From the rear of the barn came an older man with a full gray beard and worn wide brimmed hat. He walked with a limp and was heavy set.

"You the new help?" He noticed the young man eyeing his limp.

"Yes, Sir."

"Beachy said there would be a new hand helping me out. Know anything about horses?"

"Little, learned it from my Father."

"Where's your Father?"

"Been dead about three years. Most of my family is gone."

"I got the limp from the Indians. I saw ya looking at my leg. Last year they attacked the stage station at Ruby Ranch. That's where Beachy has a layover for the stage. The Indians attacked and damn near killed me—shot me in the hip. I was lucky the bullet passed through and didn't stick. Beachy sent me here until I healed. That's the story. Follow me, I'll show ya around. "Oh, yeah, I'm Sill Glass." As he spoke, Sill stuck out his large rough hand for Jacob to shake.

"Jacob Deary." Jacob returned the handshake.

"Hill Beachy has a stage leaving the hotel every day now. Two teams pull the mudwagons and it's our job to make sure it all runs smooth. Horses kept, fed, tack in order and the mudwagons ready to roll."

The two men turned and walked to the end of the barn. Sill stopped and pointed to the enclosed corner in the barn. "You can stay here if you want. Makes it easier to save some money. The tack room is dry and has a two lid stove in it."

Jacob turned and saw a stage on the other side of the barn, back in the shadows. He left Sill and walked over to it. There stood a Concord Coach. The blood-red body contrasted with the yellow running gear. It rested on two leather braces slung between the axles. Finest riding coach in the west, with its plush interior, paneled doors and a sign on the coach reading, 'Railroad Stage Line'. Jacob put his hand on the sign and rubbed it softly.

Sill came up beside Jacob. "This little beauty is Beachy's dream coach. Next year he plans to put her in service."

They walked to the barn door and Sill pulled back the wood lock. It opened into the corral. Jacob looked at the strong wooden fence on three sides and the fourth side made of stone. The creek ran through the back corner of the corral, giving the animals easy access. Up an incline on the other side of the creek was the back wall of the Idaho Hotel.

"Well, I like to think of this as my garden, but I grow and tend horseflesh. What d'ya think?"

"It all looks first class."

"It'll be just you and me tend'n' the garden. That means a lot of work with feeding, grooming, and making sure the tack is in order. We have a small blacksmith shop on the one side. A blacksmith from DeLamar comes up when we need any work done. Let me give ya a little advice. This is where the money is - horses and even cattle. The army needs the horses and the people need the food. Beachy and the army pay top dollar for a good horse. More people are moving in and they will need horses. Even the army is looking for more horses. There are wild mustang herds out in the Owyhees just waiting to be caught. Keep in mind there are Indians out there, too."

A dozen horses were in the corral. They began to move closer to the men thinking they might get a handout.

"Back, back." Sill gestured and the horses moved back.

"That's all for now. I stay up at the rooming house on Washington Street. If you need me just ask anyone up there and they will point ya to me. Time for me to go. See ya early in the mornin' - around six."

"Mr. Glass, one of the horses is lame."

Sill turned looked back to the dozen horses and saw the one Jacob pointed out.

"That's Molly. She's old and been lame for years. Never bothers her though. If you need a horse to use, take her. Don't run her hard. She will take you anywhere you want to go. Slow, but steady."

"Yes, Sir."

"Call me Sill, lad."

Jacob liked what Sill told him about the wild horses out in the mountains, his just for the picking. It caught his imagination and sounded better than working in a mine.

****

Marion Moore leaned back in the chair, balancing on its back legs. His boots rested on the porch handrail and his legs were crossed. His right hand held a tall glass of whiskey. The air was crisp and the sky clear and blue. The view from the porch overlooked Silver City and the Morning Star Mill. The new home was perched nicely on the eastern slope above the mining town.

Marion spoke in a low voice, "You built a fine home here, Colonel."

"Thank you, Marion. From here we can keep an eye on all goings on." he said with a wry smile on his face.

On a late Sunday afternoon, there were buggies going by and people walking, and the occasional clap of a hammer pounding nails.

Marion began talking about mining. "We were able to stop the Poorman Mine from taking all our gold. It ended better than I thought it would."

Dave replied, "I expected bloodshed."

Marion continued, "Everytime I think of how they swindled us out of the 'Poorman Nugget' I shake with anger. It still gets me - one 500 lb. nugget of silver and ruby crystals. You know and I know that it should have been ours. It brought more fame and money to this area than the original strike. I hate thinking about it."

Dave interjected, "Next year the Golden Chariot Mine and the Ida Elmore Mine will collide underground. I'm sure our tunnels are going to run smack into each other."

Marion paused before he replied, "You're right. I think we can hold off till after the first of the year to negotiate some neutral ground or some other idea. We want to keep our vein ours and out of their hands. Keep in mind that John Holgate is a stubborn, hard headed man. We would have better luck with the owners, but we have to go through John."

Marion had a good glow on. He asked his partner, "Dave. Why do they call you Colonel?"

"They call me Colonel Fogus cause I'm rich."

Marion objected. "I'm three times richer than you are, and they don't call me Colonel."

Dave began again. "We both are lucky we weren't shot with the outcome of the Poorman Mine. I'm glad Judge Kelly saw things our way." Moore and Fogus looked at each other and smiled. Each took a good pull on their drinks.

Smoke hung in the valley and the mountains were bare. The trees had all been harvested for mine shaft supports and firewood. On each mountainside were mines with tailing piles and large expansive mills to process the ore. Dave Fogus and Marion Moore looked out over the town and watched the evening shadows grow on Florida Mountain. The mining camp had grown into a real town. Now they had time to pause and take stock of all the changes.

A brief miners' strike had come and gone without bloodshed. Miners made $5.00 a day - the highest wages in the West, and the pay rate of the assayed ore was $5,000 dollars per ton. About 3,000 people of many nationalities were there, to strike it rich. The town was not yet civilized - no churches or schools - but the men knew they would come.

The army had established another outpost in the Owyhees, called Camp Winthrop, to keep the Indian raiding parties away from the stage lines that ran into Oregon, Nevada, and California. Now the settlers had two army camps to protect them from the Indians — Camp Lion and Camp Winthrop. A new road was being built into Silver up from a small station called Murphy and there were plans to bring the railroad to it. With the railroad close by, machinery for the mines could be shipped in and horses could be shipped out to the East.

There was talk of bringing cattle from Texas to the Owyhees - not just shipping them in, but a cattle drive - thousands of cattle, being brought 2000 miles into the Idaho Territory. Each day brought more people and more business. Marion and Dave were caught in the fast-moving stream, and they were making the best of it.

"One more drink?" Dave Fogus asked.

"Sure, why not?"

Dave poured the remains of the bottle between the two glasses. He took the water pitcher and poured a small amount into the whiskey.

"May I propose a toast, Colonel?"

"Certainly, partner."

Marion raised his glass slightly.

"May we ride on golden rails straight toward the sun. May we never see our shadows and may we become men of gold."

"You're drunk."

"That I am. Time to go. The sun is down and I have to walk back."

Marion uncrossed his leg and removed his boots from the rail. He felt the stiffness in his knees and when he stood, almost fell over. His right foot had gone numb. Slowly and deliberately, he moved toward the steps of the porch and walked down them. He turned to Dave Fogus and said, "Tomorrow."

Dave replied, "Tomorrow." Marion disappeared into the night for his unsteady walk back to the hotel.

****

The late afternoon sun shone bright and the air was hot and dry. Jacob rose before sunup and set out alone on the lame horse Molly. He rode west until the mountains dropped down into a wide, flat valley, until he found signs of wild horses. He followed the tracks down the valley and then up a draw in the mountains. He figured there were a hundred horses in the herd and that it would be a half-mile ahead. The tracks were fresh and the smell of dust hung in the air.

Jacob rode below the crest of the draw, out of sight of the mustangs. He dismounted, tied Molly off on sagebrush and quietly made his way to the crest. He got down on his hands and knees and peered over the lip. There below grazed over a hundred head of wild horses. His heart began beating faster with the excitement of the find.

He lay on the crest of the hill watching the movements of the herd. Jacob could see the back end of the draw. A rock formation on the sides and end created a box canyon. The horses moved slowly up the draw eating grass as they went.

Close to sunset, Jacob saw one black stallion stop the herd from moving into the box at the end of the canyon. This horse seemed to sense that they could be trapped. Jacob knew three men could move them up the draw into the box canyon, and could then block the escape route, leaving only enough space not to spook the horses. The horsemen could close the escape route with a makeshift fence of ropes and posts. Jacob knew his plan would work. Yes, two men on the sides of the draw and one, coming up the middle, with rope to tie off the escape route.

In a low voice Jacob said, "I'll find a way."

Jacob knew what he wanted to do. He wanted horses and acres to raise them on. He wanted a wife and sons to help him with the ranch. In an instant he knew his mission, the thing he would move mountains for. He felt his heart race and his muscles tense with the commitment.

Night came and he couldn't see the horses anymore. Quietly, Jacob crawled off the crest, stood and walked back to where Molly was tied off. He decided to spend the night without a fire and wait for sunup and see how the horses acted in the morning. He was sure they would move out of the draw at first light and move down toward the valley. They could graze there easily, and find protection in the draw at night.

FIVE

Each time fresh air entered the forge, the twin bellows groaned. With each pump the fire changed to a cherry red. John Forney used blacksmith coal, not allowing a hollow to form in the fire. He pushed coal into the center to keep it hot, and, holding the long handled pinchers tightly, pulled the horseshoe from the fire. It glowed deep red as he held it at eye level for inspection. Placing it on the anvil, he used a sledgehammer with a peen on it. For winter shoes he used a rasp to file the corked edges.

John was a man who loved working with iron. He shoed horses for Beachy and prepared the shoes for winter use. He came from the mining area just down from Booneville called DeLamar where he had a full blacksmith shop. He came to Beachy's stable on a regular basis to take care of any horseshoeing or other blacksmith work. John charged top dollar for his services because he was the best.

He worked without his shirt and the muscled arms glistened in the light from the forge. His hair fell almost to his shoulders and curled with the sweat of work. He stood six feet and looked like a man from another time - huge and primeval. The sound of the sledgehammer reverberated in the barn.

From the end of the barn, light poured in as one of the doors opened. John stopped for a moment, looked up, and waited to see who was coming in. The bright sunlight made it difficult to distinguish who the man was, but John could see someone leading a lame horse. As the figure moved forward, John made out a young man with sharp, well-defined features. The horse looked tired and rode hard. The young man removed the saddle, put the horse in the stall, and closed the gate. He went to the next stall and, filling a bucket half full of oats, Jacob returned to Molly to give her her treat.

Standing and holding the bucket, the fatigue of the last two-and-half days hit Jacob. He stopped feeding the mare for a minute, removed his hat, and whiped the dust and sweat from his forehead. Raising his head he noticed the fire-light from the forge, and heard the sharp ring of the blacksmith's hammer on the anvil. Jacob put his hat back on and walked over to the forge.

John kept pulling on the rope running to the twin hand billows. The fire glowed and roared.

Jacob saw a mountain of a man. The light from the forge shining on John's face made his features look severe.

Jacob spoke first. "Afternoon."

John nodded in reply, then spoke. "Molly looks tucker'd out."

"She is. We rode over to the valley below Baxterville."

"That's a long ride for an old, lame horse."

"Sill let me use her."

"Ah, you're the young man who works for Beachy."

"Yes."

"There's a red horse out in the corral. If you need a horse to ride, you take it. I have not been able to take her out for a ride in quite awhile. You would be doing me a favor."

Jacob replied. "Thanks. I'll take you up on it. In fact, I have some wild horses I want to round up and sell."

"When you want to use her, you just ask Iron John. If I am not here, you just call out my name before you take her, and I'll hear you."

Jacob smiled and laughed, "Anything you say."

"You plan on rounding up these wild horses yourself?"

"Well, I hadn't figured that out yet."

"Take my advice. You get two more men to go with you and use Molly as a packhorse. There's a Chinese man who works up on the upper end of Second Street. He takes care of one of the Joss Houses and cooks at the War Eagle Hotel. He's not a kid, but he's smart with horses. His name is Ah Fry. Take him with you. Any problems with Chinese?"

"No."

"There's another young man, J.C. McLafferty. He goes by J.C. Take him. He is good with horses, and honest. You can find him at the Leslie Photograph Gallery. It's south of Jordan Creek below Maize's Corral. He lives in the back. You getting' this?"

"Yes." Jacob didn't question his authority or accuracy of the information. He knew it was true.

John took a deep breath and looked at the young man. He doubted that the lad understood how much work lay ahead of him.

****

Five posts and various supplies were packed onto Molly. The lengths of rope were divided among the three men to carry. They rode most of the night and arrived at the draw in the late morning. As Jacob predicted, there were no mustangs. They rode into the draw and began their work, putting four posts across the width of the draw, and laying rope between them, ready to be raised and tied off to seal the trap. The posts were camouflaged with sagebrush and grass.

Jacob grabbed the pommel, swinging up into the saddle on his red horse. All the riders mounted and moved out. Jacob going to the lower end of the ravine. His part was to bring up the middle at the signal. Ah Fry and J.C. were to come over the crest of the ravine and keep the wild horses headed straight ahead. The two riders would appear on the crest and then ride parallel with the horses until they passed the posts. Once they got past the posts, all three men were to convene at the posts, pulling the ropes taut, leaving the horses contained in the makeshift corral. At one end, a rimrock wall and, at the other, a rope fence, were to contain the horses. There would be enough room for them to move, feed, and water without spooking.

The three men were lying flat and low to the ground looking over the crest, watching for the wild horses to move up the draw. Late afternoon moved into early evening, the temperature dropped, and the shadows became long. Jacob was first to see the herd; they moved up the middle of the ravine, with the black stallion watching for trouble. The stallion moved to the side of the draw and watched as his horses moved forward toward the protected canyon. Both nostrils flared and were held high in the air to catch any foreign scent.

Jacob waited till the horses were a quarter mile past him. He left the crest, riding slowly to the center of the draw and began waving his hat. He saw J.C. and Ah Fry on each side of the draw doing the same. Now the horses knew they were not alone. The mustangs bunched together with the stallion coming from behind to push the herd toward the box.

The horses moved at a slow trot, with the stallion at the back of the herd, pushing them forward together. Riders could be seen on both sides of the draw. J.C. and Ah Fry were watching and staying in position. The stallion was aware of the rider coming up from behind.

J.C. watched the wild horses move across the concealed ropes and into the box canyon, as Jacob drove them on, not running, just at an easy trot. Jacob came even with Ah Fry and J.C.; they came down the side of the draw, helping Jacob push the horses into the trap. The three riders spread out evenly at the fence line, quickly dismounted, and pulled the ropes taut, tying them off on the posts. All went as planned. The horses were trapped.

The stallion raised up on its hind legs and pivoted. It ran straight for the rope fence. Two mares turned and followed the stallion. All three mustangs began running at full speed for the rope fence. They were heading toward Ah Fry.

The slightly-built, gray-haired man stood frozen. His queue hung at the back of his head, his arms were outstretched and his mouth hung partially open. It looked as if the black stallion and two mares would trample the Chinese man. With one motion they jumped, clearing the fence and Ah Fry. He fell flat on his back as the horses vanished down the draw.

J.C. went over to where Ah Fry lay, looked down, and said "You're lucky they can jump."

"That was close." Ah Fry said in amazement as he sat up.

Jacob and J.C. reached down and each grabbed an arm, pulling Ah Fry to his feet. He dusted himself off and smiled.

"We got horses."

All three went to the rope fence and in the fading light looked at the herd of horses contained in their crude corral.

"How many we got, Jake?"

"Not sure. Maybe seventy, eighty head. We can count them in the morning."

Ah Fry spoke, "Now what we do with horses?"

Jacob and J.C. looked at each other puzzled. Jacob spoke: "Well, first thing in the morning we'll count them, and set a post to break the mustangs."

At first light the men awoke, ate jerky and made a fire for coffee. They collected their riding horses and Molly and went to the makeshift corral. Jacob stood on the saddle of his horse, counting the wild horses.

"I got eighty-seven by my count. Might have missed some, but not many."

"Ah Fry, I have a job for you, before we get started." Jacob went to Molly, and from a wrapped canvas he took a three-foot stick with what looked like a gigantic moccasin on one end.

"Fry, I want you to go around the outside of this whole area and stamp this into the ground." Jacob demonstrated. He took the stick and hit the ground

Silver City

with the huge moccasin. It left a mark that looked like a huge human footprint.

"You put these together so it looks like a man has been walking here. You understand?"

Ah Fry took the strange tool and hit the ground with it making a footprint. "Yes, I understand."

J.C. spoke. "What's this all about?"

"Both Indians and Whites will think Nampuh is stomping around this area and leave us be. We're going to be here for awhile, and we don't want to be looking over our shoulders wondering who's going to shoot us or steal our horses or both."

J.C. smiled and said, "I like it."

Ah Fry began walking away, stomping the ground, his horse in tow. He brushed his own footprints away with a piece of sagebrush. He returned to camp with his job completed three hours later.

Now the work began. The rest had been fun compared to getting these horses ready for a halter; the eighty-seven horses would keep them working sunup to sundown. The horses were bunched together but did not look spooked. Jacob thought there should be enough room up towards the rope fence to break them and enough space towards the back of the canyon to keep them from startling.

J.C. and Jacob walked Molly to the inside of the corral and into an open area, keeping their distance so as not to spook the horses. They unloaded a post eight feet long, then J.C. took the shovel and dug a hole for it. They slipped the post into the ground and tamped it tight. Both men leaned against the post to make sure it was secure in the ground.

Ah Fry brought his horse into the corral and mounted it. Grabbing his lariat, he worked out a large loop. J.C. took his lariat from the saddle and turned a few rounds with the loop to get the feel. Slowly both men moved toward the horses. J.C. lassoed a paint around the neck. As soon as she felt the rope, she bucked wildly. Ah Fry moved up from the side, lassoing the hind legs and pulling them out from under the horse. J.C. released his neck rope, dismounted, grabbed the halter that hung from the saddle horn and put it on the horse's head. Placing a rope around the neck, he tied a bowline knot and slipped the end through the ring under the halter. That done, J.C. took the twenty-foot length of rope and remounted his horse. Ah Fry released the loop from around the hind legs and the horse rose. He removed his lariat and led the horse around in a circle, then took it to the post and tied the end of the rope. He left ten feet of slack. The horse remained tied to the post till the following day.

At sunup the men went to the corral and untied the three horses one at a time. Their hooves were hobbled and they were led around the corral by the halter. Ah Fry took a canvas sack and rubbed it over the coat of each wild horse. Again J.C. led the horses around the corral. The men repeated this until the horses were halter-broke.

After the first few horses were halter-broke, Jacob rode to Camp Winthrop to negotiate the sale of the horses. He rode south five miles on the stage road before turning up Soldier Creek toward the camp. When he arrived, the soldiers were in formation on the parade ground. Jacob looked over the encampment. He noticed a good supply of water coming through the creek, and the protection the surrounding hills provided. A dozen log buildings of various sizes made up the camp.

Jacob stopped a soldier. "I'm looking for the Commander."

The soldier pointed toward a large log structure. "Try there."

Jacob dismounted and, tying the red horse to the rail in front of the house, he went to the door and knocked. He heard a 'Come in' from inside. He entered. Sitting at a desk on the left and in the corner sat a mustached, gray-haired man.

"I came to see about selling some horses."

The Commander looked up quickly. "You say, horses for sale?"

"Yes." Jacob replied.

"How many?"

"My count is eighty-seven. All halter broke."

The Commander spoke quickly. "I will take all of them. A twenty-dollar gold piece for each one. Of course if my Captain finds them unfit, then there will be no payment. I expect they are the local wild horses."

"Yes sir. We can bring them up to Camp Winthrop three at a time over the next few days."

"This encampment is now called Camp Three Forks."

Jacob looked puzzled and responded. "I thought..."

The Commander cut him off and said, "Politics necessitated the name change. The Eastern politicians wanted us to make our camp in the Three Forks Canyon. I tried, time and again, to let them know we would be sitting ducks down there. So I changed the name here to Camp Three Forks from Camp Winthrop and they don't know the difference. We are safe here, with good pasture, water, and timber for fire wood." The Commander smiled and looked at Jacob.

Jacob stepped out on the porch of the Commander's house. He smiled and thought the next few weeks would be busy, but he was counting his money. All three would have a good grubstake. Jacob walked down the steps, untied his red horse and pulled himself up into the saddle for the ride to the make-shift corral.

****

The three buckaroos rode up Jordan Street early on July 4, 1867. They had spent six hard weeks halter breaking the eighty-seven wild horses for the army. They were tired, hungry, and dirty. Their mounts were lean and tired. Slowly, they rode into the gaily-decorated city. Red, white and blue banners and bunting hung on all the buildings. United States flags were displayed along with the decorations.

The streets showed activity, even though it was shortly after first light. A boy stood beside the road with an unlit firecracker in his hand and a wooden match in the other. The boy had mischief written on his face. J.C. was tired and did not want any more work or activity than needed. He looked the boy straight in the eye and said, "Don't do it. Don't even think about it." The boy sensed the seriousness in J.C.'s voice. His expression changed to one of fear, and he just stood there and watched the men pass.

The city was full of ranchers and miners coming in for the Fourth of July celebration. The hitching posts were full of horses, and the stables had empty buckboards beside them, and extra horses in corrals.

Silver City

There were people in the streets a little past sunup, and patrons were already in the saloons drinking and playing cards. Silver City looked like a showgirl made up for a performance.

The men parted after crossing the bridge on Jordan Street. Jacob took the trail down behind the Idaho Hotel to the barn. He rubbed down the red horse and Molly, fed them and turned them out into the corral. Jacob was dead tired, but knew he would not sleep with all the excitement going on. For him it was a two-fold celebration, one for the Fourth of July and the other for having a leather pouch full of gold coins and a head full of dreams. Jacob cleaned himself up with a wet wash-cloth and changed his clothes.

"Where the hell you been?" Jacob was surprised by the booming voice. Sill saw the door to the sleeping area open and came in.

"Making money, Sill." Jacob took the pouch and threw it underhand to the old man. Sill scrambled to catch it.

"Well, I'll be." He threw it up and down in his large paw-like hand.

"It has a real nice weight to it. All this from the wild horses?" Sill smiled as he spoke.

Out of nowhere came a large blast shaking the barn and reverberating through the early morning air.

Jacob froze with surprise. "What was that?"

Sill was caught by surprise by the blast, then he remembered. "Oh, God. That blast is from The Morning Star Peak. Those damn fool miners take a couple of anvils and set off blasting caps on the Fourth of July. They set one anvil down and then turn the other upside down and drop it on the blasting cap. It makes a hell of noise."

Silver City

Again the deafening blast.

Jacob took back his gold pouch. "Sill, I'm going up and watch the parade, and see what's going on. I'll be at work tomorrow."

Sill nodded, and Jacob went out the barn doors and walked behind the Idaho Hotel, up the embankment by the Wells Fargo office, and onto Jordan Street. He went up First Street and to the Sommercamp Saloon. The saloon was below street level, and he walked down steps into it. The saloon was full of miners drinking and playing cards. It was a tight area with no high ceilings. The bar ran the length of the sidewall, with the potbelly stove being at the end of the bar. A number of pictures on the walls were suspended from chains that fastened close to the ceiling. There was no mirror behind the bar. A half-dozen round tables with chairs were used by the patrons to play cards. Groups of three and four were around the tables playing cards while onlookers stood at the bar, drinks in hand. Two kerosene lamps with green metal shades hung from the ceiling. At the back of the saloon was a brewery, which supplied the beer for this bar and for some of the other saloons in Silver City.

Jacob went to the bar and ordered a whiskey. He took out a twenty-dollar gold piece and placed it on the bar. The bartender raised one eyebrow. This was a large tender for a twelve-cent drink. Usually the bartender was paid with gold dust or smaller coins. Jacob felt secure with his new wealth. He was sure this was just the beginning. Jacob looked over to one of the card tables and saw J.C. playing with three other men. There was a stack of gold coins in front of him. He must be winning.

Jacob walked over to the table with drink in hand. He stood behind J.C. and tried to see his cards. J.C. had most of his hand covered but Jacob could see an ace. He looked at the other men. Two were local miners, and the other was Jim Hargrave, known locally as "Lucky Jim." Hargrave was smooth with cards and his reputation matched his skill. Jacob hoped J.C. knew the game well.

Jacob tapped J.C. on the shoulder and said, "Good luck, I'm going to watch the parade. See ya later," and left the saloon.

When he was standing on the wooden boardwalk in front of the saloon, three boys around ten years of age came up to Jacob. He had just enough booze in him to feel expansive. Reaching into his pocket he took out a twenty-dollar gold piece and gave it to one of the boys.

"You divide this with your friends."

All three boys stood looking at the gold piece in the taller boy's hand. They all responded at once, "Yes, sir." and ran off towards Smith's Drug Store on Washington Street.

Jacob walked down Washington Street, then turned down Avalanche Avenue and took a good viewing position just up from the post office. From there he could watch the parade and see the new bandstand. The air was full of the smell of freshly cut wood. He leaned back against the porch post, waiting for the festivities. The boardwalks were filling up with people dressed in their Sunday best, and the sound of a band could be heard in the distance.

The uniformed band marched by and went to the bandstand. People from the town and children followed behind, marching to the beat of the music. The women wore hats with flowers and brightly colored velvet ribbons. The people gathered around the stand and the program began. A traveling reverend led off with a prayer and the local justice read the Declaration of Independence. After the reading, the band broke into the Star-Spangled Banner. The program continued with popular songs sung by all and broken up with poems and patriotic tunes. Firecrackers went off at various times all through the program.

Following the music, the celebration took a different turn. Women in starched skirts and black shoes raced down Avalanche Street carrying an egg in a spoon. Next, the miners moved a drilling rock into place and the various crews from the surrounding mines competed to see which would drill into the rock the fastest. It was great fun for all. Jacob watched the last of the rock-drilling teams complete their hole.

J.C. came up beside Jacob and asked, "Enjoying the Fourth?"

"Yes. How'd you fare at the table?"

"Let's just say it could have been worse." J.C. smiled, shrugged his shoulders and pulled his tan hat down closer on his head. "There are some horse races down in Wagontown. Let's catch a ride and go. Whad'ya say?"

"Sounds good."

Jacob and J.C. walked to Jordan Street and went to the bridge. The first buckboard that came by they asked for a ride to the horse races. Two men were going there and said to hop on. They arrived at Wagontown and went to the large open area used for races. There was already a large crowd, with women from the saloons looking to pick up some extra business. Men talked of large bets. The track was a mile long over a flat open space. A rail fence marked off the racecourse, and a high wooden stand stood watch over the beginning and end of the race. A man stood on the stand to start and announce the winner of each race. Today there were two purses of five hundred dollars.

J.C. and Jacob became infected with the excitement. They pushed their way to the fence where they had a clear view of the start. From their position they could see Indians on the other side of the track, and some horses they intended to enter. The horses were clean and lean. One of the riders was a boy. He would be going up against experienced older men with horses.

Six horses and riders went to the starting line. A bay and black horse overshot the start line. The bay backed up, the black horse rode around behind and came up to the start again. The judge climbed to the starting stand. He raised his gun and fired. All six horses jumped and were off. The Indian boy on his smaller pinto was hidden behind the other five horses and their dust. The sound of hooves became louder as the horses passed. The Indian boy leaned forward and looked like he was talking to his horse. The bay had the lead by two lengths. Then the pinto began to move forward. The smaller animal appeared to be floating, and the black hair of the boy stood straight out behind him. The pinto seemed to be in second place and coming up on the bay. Jacob and J.C. were rooting for the Indian and his horse. The judge's hand came down as the horses crossed the finish line and the Indian boy won the purse. The men raised their hats in salute and the women clapped. The small number of Indians on the far side of the track were ecstatic. All respected the Indian boy's win.

Jacob was hooked. The people, the horses, the competition, and, best of all, the money. He turned to J.C. and announced, "The next time there are races here, I'm going to be racing."

J.C. and Jacob watched three more races before lack of sleep and six weeks of hard work caught up with them. They returned to Silver City and headed straight for their beds.

SIX

February of 1868 was cold and gray in Silver City. Soot from the coal and firewood heat had settled on the snow, making it hard and dirty. The air was stagnant and hung heavy in the valley. The exuberance of early winter was gone and fewer children skied the slopes on their handmade skis. From the pond, the rasp of the ice cutter's saw carried on the winter air. When the stage horses passed, their hooves clanked solidly with their ice shoes. Buckboards were replaced with sleighs, and the freighters used skis on their wheels to climb the steep road to the city. Residents walked the boardwalks through snow tunnels, snow piled ten feet high. There was the heavy smell of sweat in the saloons and hotels, and the valley was sunk in thick depression in the short winter days.

Tallow headlamps gave off an eerie glow, barely lighting rock surfaces. The miners went about their work with little regard for the outside world. These were hard rock miners - the toughest of the lot.

Sean set the dynamite charges in the holes after Sven drilled them. Sven manned the drill, holding the bit tight against the rock wall. His shoulders gleamed with sweat in the dim light, and patches of dirt were on his arms. They traded off work assignments during ten - hour shifts. These were hard workers; they were paid the best wages in the West.

"Sean?"
"Ya."
"Did ya say somethin'?"
"No. The drill is working on your ears."
"I heard it again. Listen."

Both men stopped working, and all movement, tuning their ears to the space around them. At first all they heard was silence, but as they stood longer, the silence turned into slight vibrations, more felt than heard. Sven set the hard rock drill down, balancing it on its brace. Both men returned to listening.

Sven spoke: "I think I hear something. Do you?"
"Not sure, but I think so."

Now, both men heard and felt the noise. Then it stopped. They did not move and returned to listening. They heard the beat of their hearts and felt the sweat drip down their chests. They looked at each other in disbelief, knowing what the noise was, and, more important, what the silence was about. In one motion they turned to run down the tunnel, but their realization was too late.

With sudden force the dynamite blast ripped into the Ida Elmore tunnel. A string of blasts came from the other side of the tunnel. The concussion threw them flat on their stomachs, while rock careened overhead, bouncing off the tunnel walls. One of the support beams broke and rock fell from the roof. Dust filled the tunnel.

A pile of rock and dirt lay in the tunnel walk. Sean and Sven were not to be seen. From where the blast came there appeared a black hole the size of a man. Then in the hole appeared a dim amber-colored light. It shone from the helmet of a miner, but not a miner from the Ida Elmore Mine.

Sean came to. He was on the ground, with rock and dust covering him. He coughed a few times before he began to move. His eyes opened and he dug himself out from under the rubble. He stumbled to his feet and began looking for Sven. He saw an arm sticking out from under the rock. He shot to the ground and furiously began digging the dirt and rock from Sven. Sven lay motionless. Sean dug the torso free, and then grabbed the big Swede's arms, pulling him out from under the rock. Once he got him free he beat on Sven's chest to get a reaction. One large gasp came. Short, struggling breaths came later. Sven would be okay.

Sven spoke to Sean. "Go, tell the boss they broke through. Leave me, I'll be all right. Go."

Sean left Sven to pull himself together and began running down the tunnel. He came to the cage shaft and gave hard tugs to the winch operator, indicative that there was an emergency, and to have the cage sent down fast. Sean stood impatiently waiting for the cage. He could hear the whine of the steam engine working the cable, and the clatter from the cage, as it came toward the fifteen hundred-foot level. The cage arrived, Sean opened the wire mess door, stepped in, and gave hard tugs on the signal line for the cage to be brought to the surface. Sean wiped sweat from his face as he moved toward the surface. He was unsure what it all meant, but he knew it wasn't good.

At the surface, the cage opened, and Sean went running toward the tool shop. Inside was the shift foreman, Myer Frank. The office doors flew open, catching Myer by surprise. He had been reviewing a tunnel map, and suddenly Sean was leaning over his desk breathless. Myer's first thought was that a tunnel collapsed and men were dead or trapped.

With urgency Myer asked, "What's the problem?"

In gasping breaths Sean replied, "They broke through."

"Who broke through?"

"Men from the Golden Chariot broke through to our tunnel."

Myer replied in a loud and angry voice, "They did what?" Myer knew what had been said. He just had a hard time believing it. Myer came to his feet and began barking orders.

"Sean, you go to the oil shack and get two more men, and meet me at the tunnel entrance. I'll bring the guns. We want to stop them where they are."

Five men walked quickly along the ore car rails down the tunnel. The mules were stopped from hauling the ore while the men made their way underground. Others, unsure what was going on, watched with curiosity. They knew it looked like trouble. The five men made it to the man cage, crammed into it, and began the trip down the fifteen hundred feet underground.

Topside, workmen began talking with each other, speculating what the trouble was. A fight of some kind must be the answer. Down below, the cage opened and the five began walking toward the workings, their lamps illuminated the shaft. They could see the rubble up ahead. As they drew closer they saw two lamps burning in the black hole. One of Myer's men pulled up his rifle and fired. The concussion was deafening. Myer Frank turned and yanked the rifle from the man's hands.

"You fool!" He looked him straight in the eye, anger and disgust on his face. Myer knew that this might be all it takes to start a war. Now, he must find a way to defuse it. He looked back at the hole in the wall.

"You men alright?" Myer waited what seemed like an eternity for a reply.

He spoke again. "Anyone over there? Anyone hurt?" Again no answer.

A runner went to town to find Marion Moore and Dave Fogus. The owners of the Ida Elmore were at the Wells Fargo office next to the Idaho Hotel, readying a shipment of bullion for San Francisco. The runner burst into the office.

"What's the fuss?" Marion spoke first.

"Mr. Moore, they broke through from the Golden Chariot!"

In a serious and low tone Moore spoke to the runner, moving closer to him. "How many?"

"Two, I think. We held them and our men are at the hole now with guns ready."

Dave Fogus spoke, "For God's sake! If this gets out of control we'll have a war on our hands."

The owners rode straight for the mine. Residents of Silver City noted the haste with which they left. Word was beginning to spread that there was trouble of some kind at the Ida Elmore and maybe another mine.

Dave Fogus and Marion Moore reached the mine shack, dismounted, and hurried in.

Marion Moore yelled, "Any of you men tell me what's going on?"

A tunnel boss turned from the window and began talking. "Mr. Moore, the miners from the Golden Chariot broke through into our tunnel. They look like they're trying to take over the mine."

Dave Fogus jumped in. "You men get some guns and sand bags and take them down to the tunnel. Don't let a man from the Golden Chariot into the tunnel. If any come through, start shooting. You understand? Stop the other shifts and have the men meet at the mine entrance."

The tunnel boss left the shack and began giving orders. Men gathered guns and walked to the mine.

Marion turned to Dave and said, "What'dya think?"

"Not sure. We got to stop it here. That's our ore they're mining. I thought we had an agreement with these men. What happened?"

On the other side of the ridge at the Golden Chariot Mine, the miners were making similar preparations. Gunnysacks were being filled with sand, guns were being collected, and the miners were preparing to protect their rights and their ore. The thirty eight-year-old mine manager and geologist, John Holgate, stood looking over the mine maps.

"For God's sake, are we off our drift line?"

He spoke to no one in particular, but it looked to him as if his measurements may be off. A change of direction of three degrees would account for the breakthrough into the Ida Elmore. John turned, went out and exited the door and walked straight to the mine entrance. He began giving orders to the miners.

After two days each mine became a fortification. At each entrance were sandbag placements with armed guards and men ready to shoot anyone trespassing. Within each of the mines, sandbags protected the fighting men at each hoisting shaft. Men with guns took up positions within the stopes and drifts.

Silver City was abuzz with the mine confrontation. Marion Moore and Dave Fogus met with their men at Fogus's home. The men crowded into the living room and the overflow stood on the front porch. A few men sat, but most of the men stood and talked with each other.

Marion Moore entered the living room and brought the group to order. "Quiet. Did ya hear me? Quiet!"

The group in the livingroom stopped their conversations and looked toward Marion. The men on the porch became quiet and leaned forward to hear.

"We are here to come up with a plan to protect our claim. Dave and I have reviewed the maps a dozen times, and the Golden Chariot is stealing our ore. They are mining our claim."

The group became animated and talkative again. Marion raised his hand and order returned.

"We want the mine to remain fortified. This means more men in front of the mine with guns. We're going to start a crew to dig below the drift. We'll dig the mine out from under them. Myer, I want you to run one of the hoses down to the opening and hook it up to the steam engine. We're going to steam the thieves out of there. You men understand what needs to be done?"

The miners spoke with one voice, "Yes", and raised their drinking glasses in salute.

Not far away, in the back room of the Clipper Restaurant, the owners of the Golden Chariot met and made plans to defend their claim. Sam Lockhart, Hill Beachy, and G.W. Grayson discussed how to keep their mine and win the Ida Elmore claim.

"Those thieves have been achin' for a fight all along." Sam Lockhart set the tone for the meeting.

Hill Beachy spoke next, "We have some legal angles we can play."

"For God's sake, Beachy, we're at war, not in court!" Sam interrupted.

"What I'm saying is that we all know each other in this town. No sense shooting our neighbors."

Grayson had been waiting for his opening and listened to Beachy and Lockhart before speaking. "Men, this could get nasty and Beachy has a point about shooting our neighbors. Our men at the mine might carry guns, but they might have second thoughts about shooting men at the Ida Elmore. They sound willing, but when it comes down to it, I think they will back off."

Beachy, with his head tilted to one side, looked at Grayson, then spoke, "What are you getting at, Grayson?"

"We need to hire some outside guns. That will take the guesswork out of whether our men will pull the trigger."

"Beachy, I'm with Grayson. He's got the right idea."

"Fellas, I've come a long way with ya. I think the best avenue is to fortify the mine with the men who work there, and do a holding action till we can get the courts involved."

Grayson looked over to Lockhart, "Think you're outvoted, Beachy. We need guns."

Beachy leaned back on the two legs of the chair and tipped his hat back on his head. He was silent, and all were quiet waiting for his reply.

"Well, boys, I'll send the word out with my stage driver in the morning. Give it a week and we should have some guns here."

Grayson leaned forward before he spoke. "One more thing. The Ida Elmore is digging a drift under our tunnel. Any ideas?"

"You bet. We'll start a shaft to meet it." Sam Lockhart was set for war.

During the next weeks, tensions ran high. An occasional shot was fired, but no targets were hit. Each mine entrance remained highly fortified, and the sheriff, A. C. Springer, refused to do anything about the warring mines, believing it was not his job to get involved. No one had placed a warrant in his hands; thus, he was legally bound not to act. Besides, the real activity was taking place underground.

In the breached shaft of the Ida Elmore, Myer Frank's whole body leaned into the pull. The hose gave way, yielding enough slack to allow Myer to maneuver it. He yelled back toward the hoisting shaft.

"Turn it on."

He moved out from behind the sandbag fortification carrying the limp hose behind him. A popping noise announced the kinks in the hose straightening out, as it filled with water. A smile appeared on Myer's face, and he uttered in a low voice, "Anyone swim?"

A shot of water jetted from the fire hose right into the breakthrough hole of the Golden Chariot. From the other side, came muffled yells and screams as men were inundated with hot water under pressure great enough to knock a man over. Myer knew the stream of water would not last much longer. Next would come a blast of scalding steam.

Listening to the screams and cussing, Myer wore a wide smile as he aimed the nozzle into the hole. He yelled behind him to shut the steam off, figuring by now they were all drowned rats. The steam faded and turned into a dribble of water.

Myer complimented the men. "Nice work, boys." Satisfaction came through his voice. "That should teach those thieves whose mine this is."

The men gave a low laugh.

Into the Golden Chariot side came the surprise of hot water and steam hitting men posted in front of the sandbag emplacements. Three of them shot to their feet and stood stunned for a moment. The blast of hot steam hit, and they all screamed and scrambled over the sandbags to safety. Water ran down the tunnel and into the shaft the miners were sinking to intersect the Ida Elmore's tunnel. The men crawled out of the hole and ran to the hoist.

"Enough of this waiting." A mud-covered miner wiped water from his face, turned to the hoist shaft and headed straight toward John Holgate.

In the mine office, John Holgate sat with his hat off, holding a cup of coffee in his free hand. His left hand held the pen to write to his family in Seattle. This was the first free moment he had had in months. It was not the kind of idle time he had ever anticipated, but work had slowed when emotions were on the rise.

The door to the mine shack was thrown open, admitting a soaked and angry miner. John looked up and asked, "What happened to you?"

"The bastards are shooting water and steam into our shaft. The tunnel is full of water, and it looks like they're planning to storm our mine."

John rose from his chair; "I'll have a look." He strode out the door and toward the tunnel. He reached the lower level, and when the hoist returned, it was filled with more men and guns. A small army of men began walking the troubled drift. John was unsure how to stop the craziness, but he needed to see the damage and what was going on.

He reached a muddy area of the tunnel and could see soaked sandbags and men. The water in the tunnel was ankle high. Reflection from the tallow lamps lit the area well. The men following John began to push forward. Complaining turned into threats and then yelling at the men on the other side of the breakthrough. John looked at the faces of his men and saw blood lust. As he began pushing forward to get to the head of the miners to take control, a shot rang out, reverberating against the tunnel walls with a deafening effect. Suddenly, more shots were fired from both pistols and rifles. John Holgate grimaced with anger. This was just what he was trying to avoid.

John yelled, "Stop! Stop your firing!"

There was no response from the men. They continued to fire at the Ida Elmore men. John was turning to look toward the breakthrough when a slug caught him high on the forehead, flipping his helmet off and taking the top of his head and brains with it. He did not know what hit him. The men behind him felt the warm mist hit them, unaware that it was blood and brains. John slumped to the ground unnoticed. The gunfire continued.

In the Ida Elmore men ran for cover, and those that had guns fired back. The sounds of gunfire and as the ping and zing of bullets were heard in the closed space. James Howard raised his rifle, fired two times, and he raised the rifle to fire a third shot, the gun suddenly fell from his right hand. He thought it strange that the gun should drop from his arm, and looking down, saw that his right arm hung oddly, as if no bone were in it. He felt a slight sting, and then noticed the red stain spreading where the elbow should be. James tried to raise his arm and found he couldn't. Then he took his left hand and grabbed it. He could feel the wound, he felt where the elbow used to be and was blown off. His arm hung limp and he could feel pain.

In a voice dipped in fear and pain he yelled, "Good God!" He began running toward the hoist to get topside.

As James passed the sandbags by the main hoist he saw Myer Frank leaning against the bags, white as death and clutching his gut with his hand. Myer was gut shot. James grabbed Myer by the collar and threw him in the hoist. Their only hope was to get out of the mine.

When word of the shootout reached Marion Moore and Dave Fogus they looked at each other and lowered their heads. They like Hill Beachy had thought legal action would win out, and the bluff would end. Now they knew that outside forces would get involved. The problem was bigger than Silver City.

****

The mine war brought in hired guns and drifters who thought they could pick up easy money working for the mines. Two such men were Enoch Fruit and John Wheeler.

Inside the Sommercamp Saloon and Brewery, John Wheeler and Enoch Fruit leaned against the bar, sipping on whiskeys. They were quiet and enjoying their drinks. They had come together looking for work, when word was spread that guns were needed. They signed on with the Golden Chariot mine to protect the mine and miners.

John Wheeler was lean with a chiseled jaw and cold gray eyes. Men knew instinctively that he was a dangerous man. Enoch Fruit always showed up where easy money could be found and he was more buzzard than man. He found ways to make money off other peoples' suffering. Wheeler blended in with other patrons of the saloon with his Western hat, suspenders, mustache and short coat. Fruit stood out. He wore a beaver skin cap and leather pants and shirt. Enoch smelled of rancid meat.

Jacob took the new buck gloves to the counter and handed them to Job Dye, co-owner of the general merchandise store. The new store had been built with Dye's partner, T. J. Butler, and they had been in business for over a year. Each time Jacob went to the store he found more people shopping. Silver City was booming, with a growing population and new businesses to meet the demands. It was becoming more civilized and losing the rough edges of a mining town.

Jacob handed Job the three dollars and fifty cents for the gloves, "Thanks."

"Welcome, Jacob. Have a good evening."

Jacob exited the granite building and walked down Washington Street, back to his lodging at the barn, turning his collar up against the cold. The mud on the street was beginning to freeze. Jacob thought it would be cold tonight.

He started to turn down First Street and looked up at the horses tied to the rail on Washington Street — probably the customers of the Sommercamp Saloon. His eye went over to a pinto horse. Strapped onto its saddle was a scabbard. Jacob saw the stock of a rifle, and knew it for his rifle stolen by the Indians. He walked over between the horses and ran his hand over the stock. He felt every nick and scratch, and then he ran his finger over the back of the trigger guard. Engraved in the metal were the initials PD. His father, Philip Deary, had engraved the rifle when he bought it. He had given the rifle to Jacob before he died. The blood rushed to Jacob's face.

Jacob walked through the double doors and down the steps into the saloon. At the bottom of the steps he stopped.

"Who owns the pinto outside?" He spoke in a loud, firm voice. The bar room fell silent. Jacob stood and waited.

Enoch gave Wheeler a sideways glance and then looked back to the young man. He could not figure why the man was looking for him. He paused and then spoke, "It's my horse, lad."

Jacob looked at him; "You have a rifle on that horse that belongs to me."

Enoch went from leaning his two forearms on the bar to slowly standing up and turning toward Jacob. He smiled and then gave a low laugh. His rotten teeth showed as he spoke, "How could that be? I just arrived in Silver and that rifle has been mine for years." Enoch continued to smile, while John Wheeler turned a quarter turn toward Jacob and slid his right hand down toward his ivory handled revolver.

"That rifle was stolen from me by Indians three years ago. My father, Philip Deary, gave it to me. You look on the trigger guard and you'll find the initials PD."

The smile disappeared from Enoch Fruit's face. He knew they were locked in a fight. Enoch could see the set jaw of the young man. One of the saloon patrons went out the entrance and quickly returned.

"The lad is right. There is an engraved PD on the Springfield rifle."

Enoch said. "You say'n' I'm a liar?"

The saloon patrons moved from the tables to the side of the room. Those who might be in the line of gunfire moved out of the way.

Jacob replied, "I'm say'n that's my rifle and I mean to take it."

Hill Beachy stopped his card game and moved to the side of the room. Jacob did not see him. Hill knew the two customers at the bar were tough. Jacob might have a chance with one, but not with both. Beachy edged his way to the bar and came up behind and beside John Wheeler. Beachy quietly removed his Colt from his holster and put the barrel in Wheeler's side.

Enoch knew that Wheeler would cover him and back him with any story. He moved away from the bar and toward the center of the saloon, sliding his right hand to his knife in the sheath on his back right hip. Jacob could not see the knife from where he was standing and Enoch knew Jacob was unarmed.

"Can't let ya take my rifle, lad. You want to continue this, I'm game."

He could hear the resolve in Enoch Fruit's voice. Jacob was ready, and committed to getting his rifle back. Enoch began moving toward Jacob in a slow walk with his right hand partially hidden behind his back. Jacob figured a knife would come into play. He eyed a chair close by that he could grab and throw up between the knife and him.

"Well, lad, you can walk out and nobody will think less of you." As he spoke, Enoch continued his slow walk toward Jacob. Enoch smiled.

Jacob spoke, "Not today."

Both men knew the talk was over. Enoch moved two more steps forward before making his move. Like a cat, Enoch pulled the knife from behind his back and lunged toward the opponent. Jacob moved sideways and in one motion grabbed a chair, flinging it between the knife and him. The knife caught the edge of the chair and glanced off.

Enoch regained his balance and came for Jacob. Jacob backed up toward the door. Enoch swung the knife, and Jacob moved back quickly and up the steps. His back rested against the entrance door and Enoch planted his feet for the final thrust, but before Enoch struck his target Jacob leaned back against the door, it gave way, he stumbled to the right and found himself out and standing on the street. He was on the short narrow extension of First Street known as Dead Mans' Alley.

In the street, Jacob kept his balance. Enoch lunged again toward his prey. Jacob moved to the side, swung with his right fist and caught Enoch a solid blow in the jaw. The right arm and shoulder were stronger since the gun shot wound. The force of the punch surprised Enoch. He gathered himself and swung wildly with the knife. Again a punch hit his eye. Enoch felt warm liquid falling into his eye and blurring his vision. Again and again he wielded the knife, hoping to catch the young man with the sharp long blade. Each time Jacob pivoted to the side, and at last he hit Enoch squarely in the nose. Blood gushed forth and Enoch let out a yell of pain. Again Jacob hit the man, and this time he went down on his knees. Jacob did not wait for him to recover, and came full force with his fist under the jaw. The teeth hitting each other sounded like glass breaking, and over Enoch Fruit went. He stared blankly at the sky. Jacob went to the man, put his right boot on his right arm, and removed the knife from his hand.

Jacob had not noticed the crowd till now. He heard his own rapid deep breathing, and looked around at the crowd. No one said a word. Jacob staggered backwards, turned, went to the pinto horse and removed the Springfield rifle. He started back to the barn.

Inside the saloon the crowd began pouring back in and up to the bar to celebrate the brawl and discuss the excitement. John Wheeler was still at the bar with his back to Hill Beachy.

Beachy spoke quietly: "I'll tell ya what I'll do. I'm gonna slip out the back door—all the time watching you. If you turn around before I leave, you're a dead man. Understand?"

John Wheeler nodded his head in understanding.

"We'll just call this a friendly evening. If ya want to make more of it, just let me know."

Hill Beachy backed out the rear door with the Colt in his hand.

****

On March 30, 1868, the local newspaper—The Avalanche—reported that the war between the Ida Elmore Mine and the Golden Chariot Mine had ended. Governor Ballard sent a proclamation with a marshal calling for an end to the warring. The proclamation was presented to both parties and they agreed to come to terms. By 2:00 a.m. on Monday morning the two mines reached an agreement. A holding company was established to manage the property fifty feet north and south of the main shaft. The deeds and agreements were signed, and the warring mines put away their guns.

By April 4, 1868, Silver City returned to normal. The tension was out of the air and the residents were working at becoming neighbors again.

Marion Moore and his friend, Jack Fisher, were coming from the Smith Drug Store and walking down Avalanche Street toward the Wells-Fargo office. Marion Moore planned to leave town on the stage and travel to Idaho City.

"When ya coming back?" Jack asked.

"A couple of weeks. Looking forward to getting out of town. It's been a long month." Marion replied.

Both men walked toward the Wells-Fargo office and began crossing Jordan Street.

Sam Lockhart sat in the captain's chair on the front porch of the Idaho Hotel. He had left the hotel saloon for some fresh air; the last hand of cards were stale. He needed to clear his head of the whiskey and

Silver City

poor luck. He saw the two men come down Avalanche Street and angle toward the Wells-Fargo office. As they began to cross Jordan Street, Lockhart's anger began to rise. Sam Lockhart had just enough whiskey in him; that he could not keep his mouth in check.

"You two slime-balls leaving town after you stole our mine?"

Marion Moore and Jack Fisher froze in their steps and looked at each other in disbelief. They both turned to looked at Sam Lockhart and could see that the whiskey was doing the talking. Both men resumed walking toward the stage office.

"I'm talkin' to you two."

Jack Fisher and Marion Moore glanced sideways toward Sam Lockhart. They did not want trouble. Lockhart moved his right hand toward his gun and Moore and Fisher froze, reached for their holsters, and pulled out their pistols. At the same time Lockhart fielded his pistol in a sitting position, aimed and fired. The first slug caught Jack Fisher high in the thigh and tore a nasty wound. Marion pulled his gun up, bent his knees and fired two shots. Both shots of Moore's were high and slammed into the hotel. Lockhart fired two more shots. One shot went over the head of Fisher as he fell, and the second caught Marion Moore high in the chest. The slug hit flesh and bone. For a moment, Marion Moore stood frozen in disbelief and then began running toward the Oriental Restaurant, firing one more shot at Lockhart. The shot was far off the mark. Moore ran ten more steps and collapsed.

Sam Lockhart stood up out of the chair, breathing hard from the gunfight. He turned and went into the hotel. Miners close to the windows in the saloon watched wide-eyed. Lockhart stood in the hotel entranceway on the other side of the doors. His men from the saloon came to him with guns drawn to support him in his battle.

Store owners and city people pulled the two wounded men from the street and onto the porch of the Oriental Restaurant. One yelled out, "Get the doctor."

Marion Moore was taken to Dave Fogus's house where he remained conscious and alert through the night and the following day. Again tensions ran high in Silver City, with the supporters of Moore looking for revenge, and supporters of Sam Lockhart protecting him.

Jacob Deary visited Marion Moore the day after the shooting, to say his goodbyes. Marion Moore died a few hours later.

SEVEN

"Iron John? Do you have a horse I may ride in the Fourth of July race?"

John Forney leaned back on his heels and crossed his large muscular arms and thought for a moment.

"Well, yes. That white horse out in the corral is fast. It's one of Beachy's favorites, but I gave it to him so I have loaning rights." His broad smile made creases in his face.

"Thanks." Jacob returned the smile.

He went to the tack room and took down a bridle, scooping a couple of helpings of oats and putting them in an oats bag. As Jacob walked into the corral the horses moved away from him. In the far end of the corral the white horse stood beside the rock fence. Jacob walked slowly toward the horse with oat bag out in front. The horse did not startle and Jacob let him nuzzle into the bag for the oats. He took the bridle and gently placed it over the horse's head, placing the bit in his mouth. At first, the horse raised its head in objection, but then complied. Jacob took hold of the mane and easily swung up on the horse's back in one fluid motion, using his heels on the horse's side. It began a half trot and the two made a trip around the corral without trouble. Jacob knew they would make a great team at the Fourth of July race that was three weeks away.

Race day came, and J.C. McLafferty flew into the barn, walking through the door into the room where Jacob slept. Jacob opened up one eye and looked up.

"What's up?"

"Jacob, we need to get going."

Jacob sat up, looked at J.C. sideways, took a deep breath, got out of bed, went to the chair where his clothes were, and began putting them on.

Jacob spoke, "I want you to go up to the Idaho Hotel and place a bet with the bartender. He's the only honest gambler in town. You take my poke and bet it all on my white horse. You understand? I have two thousand dollars in there." Jacob pointed to the leather pouch on the edge of the chair. "When I win, we'll have enough for us to go into the livestock business together. You pool your money with mine and we'll make even more money. You game?"

"Sure." J.C. spoke with assurance and enthusiasm. They both had talked of having their own place to run cattle and raise horses. Now it was so close they could taste it.

J.C. went to the hotel saloon and spoke to the bartender in a quiet voice, then handed him two leather pouches with drawstrings. J.C. left the bar, heading for the racetrack in Wagontown.

Jacob rode the white horse to the track, slow enough to loosen the muscles of the horse, but not enough to tire it out. Since he was early for the race, he tied the white horse to a wagon wheel behind the starting stand and climbed up on the fence. He watched people filling the stands and climbing the mountainside for a birdseye view of the racetrack. The women wore elegant long dresses and carried parasols, and the stands were decorated in bright patriotic colors.

Jacob watched the first races, but his mind and gut were on his own race. He did not know whom he was running against: all he knew was that he had to win. The time for his race came and Jacob climbed down from the fence. He went to the white horse, checked the cinch and rubbed the horse's neck, then gracefully pulled himself into the saddle. He reigned left and headed for the starting line.

Jacob drew the number two position for the half-mile race. He would have preferred a shorter race, but the purse for this one was larger - two thousand dollars for the winner. He brought his horse to the line, holding the reins tightly. Each muscle of the horse flexed and became charged for the competition. Jacob was unsure whether he could hold him at the line. The other horses took their position.

Jacob glanced down the line of horses and riders and saw the lone Indian boy on his pinto. A pang of fear caught Jacob before he could shake it off.

He held the horse against the rope, keeping it from exploding out. He heard the gun, the rope dropped and in one motion his horse leaped from the start line. The white horse was half a length ahead of the other six horses at the opening. Jacob was frozen in the moment working to do his job. He leaned over the right side of the neck, whispering to the horse. He lay flat down on the saddle and used his heels to push his mount to even faster speeds. No other horse or rider was distracting or challenging the white horse.

The crowd began to roar as the riders came to the half - way point. The white horse led the field, with the pinto horse three quarters of a length back. The rest of the horses were two lengths back in a tight knot vying for third place. The crowd became louder as the fight for first and second place became unsure. The sentiments were with the White man, but everyone's heart respected the Indian boy and his challenge for first place.

Jacob was oblivious to the noise of the crowd. He did sense a challenge. It was the rising noise of hooves. Then in his peripheral vision he caught sight of a horse moving up. The challenger was the pinto carrying the Indian boy. For the first time in the race the thought of losing came into his mind.

Jacob looked straight ahead, pushing the thoughts and the image of the Indian boy out of his head. He gritted his teeth, leaned forward, and talked to the horse.

"Give me all, now."

The pinto was almost even with the white horse. Only a few strides kept the pinto from gaining the lead. The finish line was in sight, and Jacob crouched lower against the white horse and drove his heels into the horse's flanks. They intended to be first.

The pinto seemed frozen in motion beside the white horse - not gaining or loosing momentum. Then the white horse moved a half-stride further ahead. Jacob sensed they were pulling away from the Indian boy and his pinto. The white horse and Jacob were across the finish line. He reined back on it, bringing it to a trot and then to a walk. They could hear the roar of the crowd. On the right side the pinto trotted by, and Jacob met the eyes of the Indian boy. The boy nodded congratulations, then turned his horse and went to his people.

Jacob rode to the judge's stand and collected his two thousand dollars. As he stood looking at the currency, J.C. came up and spoke. "We have money. I put my money and yours on the white horse."

Jacob looked at J.C., gave a wide smile and laughed. "We're going into the horse and cattle business."

"Congratulations on the race!" J.C. gave a look of approval.

****

J.C. and Jacob rode North of Silver City and downstream from Cow Creek to the ranch of Con Shea. Con Shea had brought longhorns from Texas into the Owyhees the year before, in 1867. He was working as a miner when he was approached by Christopher Moore to bring the beef to the Owyhees. A Madam from a local brothel grubstaked Shea for the adventure, and he drove the cattle through Indian country and the open West to bring food to the miners.

The two young men came to this man who had land to lease and cattle to buy. They agreed on a parcel of land that was west of Silver City, close to old Baxterville, or, as the new name says - Jordan Valley. Jacob and J. C. knew they could work together and grow their herd. They were good with horses, and they knew cattle. The wild mustangs could be sold to the army and to Eastern markets, and the beef to miners.

Jacob and J.C. returned to Silver City at the end of July, 1868. They came to pack their belongings and head out. Before leaving, Jacob went to the Idaho Hotel saloon to see Hill Beachy and thank him for the work and lodging.

"Well, Jacob, we're going to miss ya. You did good work for the stage line."

"Thanks. I appreciate it all."

Jacob stuck out his hand and Hill Beachy returned the handshake.

"By the way, Jacob, did you hear that Mercy Eastman passed away?"

"No. What happened?

"Mercy and her baby died of Puerperal Fever."

"They were real good to me. Sorry to hear it." Jacob turned and headed for the door.

Jacob hadn't told J.C. yet, but there was one thing more needed before the cattle business was to begin. Jacob needed a good horse.

He went down to the stables one last time. John Forney was in the back on his weekly blacksmith tour. John put down his hammer and braced his fists on his hips when he saw Jacob come in.

"Iron John, I need a horse."

"Odd you should ask. Happens that I have one for you."

Jacob looked surprised by the reply.

"There is a black horse in the corral with your name on it. It is a wild mustang that I bought. It is broke, but tough to handle."

Jacob went to the stable door and opened it. He looked out into the corral and saw the black horse. Instantly, he knew the horse. It was the one that got away when they were mustanging. Jacob smiled with excitement. He walked back to John Forney.

"Thanks, John."

"Anytime, Jacob."

Sill Glass opened the large barn doors and looked toward the back. He saw two men back by the forge and walked to them.

"Hear you'r leaving town to get rich." Sill spoke and smiled.

"You bet."

"Take care." Sill stuck out his rough large hand. Jacob shook the proffered hand.

EIGHT

The whine of mosquitoes reverberated in John Wheeler's ears. He pulled down his hat and tucked his coat collar closer to his neck. He sat cross-legged and kept his hands protected up under the sleeves of his heavy coat, the repeating rifle resting in the crook of his arm. Occasionally, he would shake his head and the insects would rise and create a buzz.

Before sun up at Massacre Flats he had tied his horse close to the canyon entrance, making sure no one saw him move into the valley along Reynolds Creek. Wheeler had positioned himself in the willows close to the stage road and had hunkered down.

He waited for the Silver City stage with the intent to rob it and to settle some old scores. After the mine battles were over and the town had returned to normal, John had stayed around the saloons, playing cards. He mostly won, but four days earlier a gambler ran the table and cleaned him out of all his winnings and pay for being a hired gun. The gambler had cheated him, and he aimed to get what was his. At the same time, he could pay back Hill Beachy for interfering with the fight. He could steal the passengers' fat pokes and take the bullion on board the stage. Wheeler would collect what was his and then disappear into Oregon. If it came to killing, he was ready. John Wheeler did not want trouble, but he was not shy about defending himself. By late morning the stage would be making the turn out of the flats and heading up the pass. He would strike just before the driver made the turn.

****

Bill Anderson left Silver City before first light, heading for Boise City to pick up supplies for the carpentry job he worked on in town. Two horses pulled the wagon and he rode comfortably with the empty wagon. His elbows rested on his thighs with the reigns lightly held in each hand, and the horses were surefooted and reliable.

Bill was lean and of average height, with skin that looked like dark tea from working outside all summer, and lines in his face making him look older than his thirty years.

He entered the far end of the valley about mid-morning and drove the wagon a few more miles before he decided to stop and wait for the other traveler to pass through Massacre Flats. Bill did not have a gun with him. He did not own one, and would have been hard - pressed to hit anything even if he did. Gently, he reined the horses to the left, pulled off the road and made ready to rest, graze and water them. It would give him time to catch a bite to eat and wait for fellow travelers.

Bill took the harnesses off his two horses, letting them water and graze close to the wagon. He took a cloth bag and canteen from the wagon, sat down on the ground and leaned back on the rear wheel. From the bag he took two hard rolls filled with meat and began eating. The first mouthful swallowed hard, and he needed water to wash it down. The shade from the wagon felt good and a light morning breeze washed over him. He figured it would not be long till someone or the stage came by, and he would have a companion to travel with through Massacre Flats.

Suddenly the horses whinnied, moving backward quickly, and then ran down the creek toward the canyon entrance. Something had spooked them. As he watched, a pang of fear hit his gut. He would have to walk into the mouth of danger to retrieve his horses. This he did not like.

Stiffly he rose to his feet, reached into the wagon for a length of rope. Cautiously he began walking in the direction of the horses. He could see them a half-mile ahead. It would take time to round them up and bring back to the wagon.

Anderson walked along the stage road, keeping his horses in sight. They had stopped running and were grazing by the willows. He left the road and moved toward them. Suddenly, from across the creek came a group of Indians with paint and feathers. For sure they saw him! Anderson froze in his tracks and watched as three Indians ran toward him.

"Surely, I am done." he thought.

A giant of an Indian, Nampuh, was 50 yards away and running directly toward Bill, who crouched down behind a ledge of rocks and waited for his fate. In his thoughts he said goodbye to those he loved. It would not be long before his blood-dripping scalp would be hanging from Nampuh's belt.

But Nampuh made straight for the road. Bill looked back over his shoulder and saw the stage coming, full of passengers. Anderson felt relief for the moment. He was not the object of the Indians' attention. The second Indian, next to Nampuh, was nearly opposite his hiding place, and again he thought he would be discovered.

As Anderson watched the Indians, a crack from a rifle startled him. He watched in disbelief as the Indian closest to him fell dead only 20 yards away. Nampuh jumped behind a large rock and the third Indian ran back across the creek and was not seen again.

The stage driver, Charley Barnes, held the reigns of the four horses tightly in his hands. He looked ahead and took a deep breath as he prepared to enter Massacre Flats. Charley was no stranger to trouble, but even he was surprised to see three Indians running across the creek. He realized if they kept coming at that pace, they would be able to jump the stage before he made the turn. He heard the crack of a shot and watched as one Indian fell dead, one ran back over the creek, and the other huge Indian made for the large rock. Then Charley saw the White man hiding behind the low ledge. Somehow it didn't all add up. It made no difference, and he gracefully put the silk to the horses. The mudwagon swiftly climbed out of the flats and over the pass. On board the stage were Judge Roseborough, Charley Douglas the gambler, and Mrs. Record and her daughter. The driver was doubtful that the passengers knew of their risk, or of the drama that was unfolding outside.

Bill Anderson stayed unmoving and watched the stage disappear. He watched the Indian Nampuh carefully crawl from one end of the rock the other, then peer around it. Nampuh was unsure where the mystery shot came from. The Indian put his ear to the ground to listen for any movement. Next, he tied sagebrush to his back and slowly began crawling away.

Bill Anderson watched as the huge man began crawling directly toward him.

Anderson formed a plan to jump and run toward the willows that Nampuh watched, with the hope that another White man was hiding there. He knew that if he waited much longer, Nampuh would see him. Then when Nampuh was half the distance between the rock and the ledge behind which Anderson hid, a voice rang out.

****

The late July morning was gaining heat. John Wheeler watched from his hiding place as two horses came running down the valley, slowed and began grazing. A half-hour later a man with a light blue shirt and tan hat came walking down the stage road toward the horses. Further back, Wheeler could see the dust and just the top and driver of the stage coming. His plan was getting more complicated and he didn't like it.

Suddenly, from the right, three Indians dashed at full speed out of the willows. All three were painted and feathered. One large Indian could be no other than the infamous Nampuh. Robbing the stage moved quickly out of Wheeler's head. He knew he could not fight a two-front war. He quickly made the decision to attack rather than to wait to be found. From his sitting position, he raised his rifle and got a bead on Nampuh. As Wheeler pulled the trigger the Indian running closest to the chief crossed between the two, and caught the bullet square in the back. Instantly, the Indian was down and unmoving. Nampuh jumped behind a large rock. All was silent. The third Indian crossed the creek and disappeared over the rise.

Still sitting cross-legged, John Wheeler sat waiting and watching. The stage driver whipped his horses and the stage jumped with added speed, turning the corner and quickly climbing toward the pass and out of sight. Wheeler sat amused that this did not turn out anything like he had planned. Now he must continue the fight.

He knew the White man was behind the ledge close to the road, and that Nampuh could not move from behind the rock without exposing himself. He saw the sagebrush move. A slight smile broke out on Wheeler's face. Slowly Wheeler rose to his feet. The smile was gone, his jaw was set, and he yelled from the willows, "Get up from there, Nampuh, you old feather-headed, leather-bellied coward!"

Nampuh felt the anger rise from his gut. He sprang up and leveled a large double-barrel rife at the willows and said, "You coward, me no coward! You come out, I'll scalp you too!"

At this Wheeler jumped from the willows and into view.

"Here I am, now sail in, old rooster!"

Both men fired their weapons at almost the same time. Anderson watched as Nampuh staggered, then recovered, and fired again. Nampuh threw the gun down and began running toward his dead companion. Wheeler fired again and a slug slapped into Nampuh. He continued running, reached the dead Indian, grabbed his gun, and turned and fired toward Wheeler. His response was too late. John Wheeler fired another unerring shot into that powerful Indian.

Nampuh staggered, then regained his balance and pulled his knife, giving a blood-curdling whoop and starting toward Wheeler. Wheeler fired shot after shot into the charging Indian. He kept coming. Wheeler held his ground and kept firing into the Indian, his face frozen with resolve. Anderson watched in fear as the Indian came closer to his enemy, still unsure who would win. Maybe Nampuh would reach Wheeler and crush him with his grip.

Thirty yards away the Indian fell, his leg broken, never to rise again. Wheeler emptied his gun into the Indian. When all sixteen shots were used, he reloaded. From where he stood John Wheeler called out, "How do you like the way my gun shoots, old Hoss? I'll bet my scalp against yours that you don't scalp any more White men in this canyon soon!"

Nampuh cried out in English, "Don't shoot me anymore, you have killed me!"

Wheeler walked up close to the Indian and pulled out his ivory handled revolver, paused for a moment, then called out to Anderson.

"Come down, whoever you are. There is no danger now."

Bill walked down to where the Indian lay. He looked at the huge man and counted twelve bullet wounds. Both legs and one arm were broken. Nampuh asked for water, and Wheeler replied, "Hold on until I break the other arm, then I will give you a drink."

The Indian replied, "Do it quick and give me a drink, and let me die."

Wheeler leveled his pistol and fired one round into the arm. It fell limp and useless. He went to the willows and brought up his canteen full of water and placed it in the mouth of the Indian. He drank it all. Nampuh then wished he had some whiskey. Wheeler said he carried some for medicinal purposes and told

Nampuh he could have it if he thought it would do him any good.

Nampuh replied, "Get it quick, for I am going blind".

Wheeler got the pint flask and gave it to him. The Indian drank every drop, and then saying, "I am sick and blind" he fell back, apparently dead. After a few moments, he seemed to revive, saying he felt better. He asked the two White men to wash the paint and dust from his face and see what a fine looking man he was. They complied with his request, and to their surprise found a fine looking face, with the handsomest set of teeth they ever saw. He had large, black, wicked eyes and tanned skin. His hair was long and black, and leaned toward being kinky. He was of enormous size and neither Anderson nor Wheeler had ever seen anyone so large and strong.

Nampuh became talkative and expressed a wish that the men make him one promise. Wheeler asked what the wish was. He asked not to be scalped or taken to Boise City after he died, but to be dragged in among the willows and to have some rocks piled upon him, and his old gun laid by his side.

"If you will promise me this, I will die satisfied," he said. Wheeler told him that if he would tell him who he was and where he came from, he would perhaps promise to do what he wished; but that he must answer all the questions he was asked, and tell the truth. Nampuh agreed, and began talking in a low voice.

"I have been a very bad man, and if I tell you all that I have done, I am afraid you will not do what I have asked of you."

Wheeler said, "I have been assured by many prominent citizens of Boise City that if anyone killed you and brought your feet and your scalp to Fort Boise that at least $1000 would be paid for them. You have done a great deal of mischief, killed many White people and everybody thinks you were one of the party that killed Mrs. Scott and her husband on Burnt River last fall. Your big tracks were found the next day near the scene of the murder, as they have always been found when Indians killed White people in this part of the country. I know that you have been a bad man, but if you will tell me everything, I will not tell anyone that you are dead, nor tell anything about you."

Nampuh began, "I was born in the Cherokee nation. My father was a White man, Archer Wilkinson; He was hanged for murder in the Cherokee nation when I was a little boy. My mother was part Cherokee and part Negro, I was told. She was a good Christian woman. My name is Starr Wilkinson. I was thus named after Thomas Starr, a noted desperado in the nation. The boys always made fun of me because I was so large for my age. I had a bad temper and got to drinking when quite young, and got to be so strong that when anyone would call me a nickname I would fight him. In this way I came near killing several with my fists. I found out that I would soon be killed if I remained in that country so I ran away from home and went to Tilaqua, then the capital of the Cherokee Nation. There I fell in with some emigrants who were going to Oregon in 1856, and drove a team for my board across the plains. The folks I traveled with were very kind to me. I fell in love with a young lady of the company, who thought a good deal of me until we fell in with a train from New York. Along with these new people was an artist, who was a smart, good-looking fellow. He soon cut me out. After this the young lady would hardly notice me or speak to me. I knew then that he had told her something bad about me. He made fun of me several times, and while we were camped near Goose Creek Mountains he and I went out one morning to hunt up the stock. We went to the bank of the Snake River. I asked him what he intended to do when he got to Oregon."

"He said he was going to marry my girl and settle down. I told him he should not do so, for I thought I had the best right to her. He laughed at me and said, 'Do you suppose she would marry a big nigger like you and throw off a good-looking fellow like me?' This made me mad and I told him I was no Negro and that if he called me that again I would kill him. So he drew his gun on me and repeated it again. I was unarmed but started at him. He shot me in the side but it did not hurt me much, so I grabbed him and threw him down and choked him to death, then threw him into the Snake River. I took his gun, pistol and knife, and ran on into the hills."

"The emigrants did not leave camp for a few days. They were perhaps hunting for me. Some of them went on to Oregon, but the family that I had been traveling with went back with some others to Salt Lake, where they wintered. I made my way to the Boise River, where I found a French trader and trapper, a man named Joe Lewis, who had been with the Indians for many years. This Joe Lewis was one who helped massacre Doctor Whitman and many others near old Fort Walla Walla in 1847. He was a bad man, but he was a good friend to me when I needed a friend. So I went with him and joined the Indians, and have remained with them ever since."

"In 1857, I went with Lewis and some Indians near the emigrant road for the purpose of stealing stock from the emigrants. In one of our raids I found cattle that I knew had belonged to the family I crossed the plains with the year before. So I determined to go to the train and see if my girl was with them. I found her, but she was very mad with me, as were all the rest. They said they thought I had killed Mr. Hart, the young artist, and that I ought to be hanged for it. They told me to leave the camp. I told the girl that if she did not have me she would be sorry for it before she got to Oregon. I had to leave, but was determined to have revenge, so I took Joe Lewis and 30 Indians and followed them down the Boise River to where it empties into the Snake River and massacred them and ran off all their stock. I and several Indians ravished the girl before we killed her. I am sorry for that now, for she was a good girl, but it is too late now to be sorry. I was mad and foolish."

"I have been in several other massacres. I helped to kill that Scott family on the Burnt River. We wanted their horses. I killed a lone traveler near where I lay. He was between us and robbing the stagecoach. We took his horse and belongings. I also helped to kill an officer and took his wife prisoner last fall. The officer was on his way to Camp Lyon. His wife, sick, had a child and could not ride, so some of the Indians killed her. I had a squaw for a wife, and when Jeff Stanford was out with a lot of men fighting us, they killed my wife and carried off my little boy. Since that time I have done all the mischief I could, and am glad of it."

Wheeler and Anderson stood silent. Wheeler cocked his head and asked, "What became of Joe Lewis?"

Nampuh responded: "He was shot by a man who carried the express from Auburn to Boise in 1862. Lewis was trying to steal some horses on the Payette one night. The expressman shot across the river with buckshot, hitting Lewis in the side and wounding me in the leg. It was dark, and neither of us spoke. The expressman did not know anyone had been hit."

"Joe whispered to me," continued Nampuh "that he was hurt bad, so I took him on my back and started to run with him, but he soon died and I covered him up in the sand on the bank of the Payette, where he was never found by the Whites; and that was the last of poor Joe, and I hope you will do that much for me."

Wheeler said, "All right, Mr. Wilkinson; guess I will do it, for I am from the Cherokee nation myself, and have a little Cherokee blood in my veins. I will not refuse your dying request."

Nampuh replied, and, as he spoke, tears came to his eyes. "You are a brave man and I know you will keep your word. I am a brave man, too, and you shot a little too quick for me, and you had the best gun and you have killed me. Your shot struck me just as I was pulling the trigger, else I should have killed you, as I hardly ever miss anything I shoot at. I got my old gun in a massacre in 1857. I do not know how many men I have killed with it. I knew I was killed when your first shot struck me, for I could not see to shoot well afterwards."

Nampuh began throwing up blood and the red fluid continued to run from his wounds. He was possessed of so much vigor and vitality that he lived for nearly two hours after receiving so many mortal wounds.

Wheeler asked where the Indians got their ammunition. He said that some of it was obtained from friendly Indians who visited the towns and military posts for that purpose. Nampuh continued:

"Nearly all of my little band of warriors are killed off. There are but five left, who have been running with me. You have just killed one of the bravest of the band. He has been one of my head braves ever since the Indians recognized me as the leader of their band. His father is the old medicine man, and he told me when we left not to go on this trip, for he had dreamed about us. He dreamed that there was a large snake secreted in the bluffs that had a White man's head, and had a medicine gun, that when he pointed it at the Indians they could not see how to shoot, and that after killing them he broke their guns to pieces. He wept when we left camp, and said that he would never see us again, until we met in the spirit land, and I see now that he was right. If I had minded him, I would not have got killed."

Wheeler said, "Well, if you meet the old medicine gentleman in the spirit land, tell him he was a good hand at dreaming, even if he did call me a snake."

Wheeler then asked where the rest of the Indians were camped?

Nampuh replied, "This is something I cannot tell, but I will tell you anything else you may ask me. There are but few of them left and now that we are killed, the rest will soon go into the fort, and it would do you no good to kill them."

"The little band I run with call themselves 'Paiutes'. The rest call themselves 'Fish Indians' because they live by fishing on the Malheur and Snake Rivers, and do not mix with the Lake Paiutes and Bannocks. The other Indians are not friendly with us, and I care nothing about them, but our little band have been brave Indians. They have always treated me well, and I do not wish to betray them as the last act of a bad life."

Wheeler said, "Bully for you, Wilkinson. I think more of you than I did before, for you are not a traitor, if you have been a bad man otherwise."

Wheeler asked him how tall he was and how much he thought he weighed.

"I do not know, for I have grown very much since I joined the Indians. When I left the Whites I was but 19 years old, then I measured 6 feet 6 inches in height and weighed 255 pounds."

"I must weigh at least 300 pounds now."

Anderson looked at the dying Indian's frame and noted that there was not an ounce of fat on him and that he was a model of strength and endurance. From his pocket Anderson took a tapeline and rule. He took the exact measurements of the Indian. Around the chest fifty-nine inches, height six feet eight and one-half inches, around the ball of the foot, eighteen inches, length of foot seventeen and one-half inches, around the widest part of the hand eighteen inches. Anderson estimated that Nampuh weighed at least three hundred pounds.

Anderson asked if he knew how strong he was.

Nampuh replied, "No, but I was very powerful. I had as many as 10 Indians at me, trying to throw me down but they never succeded. I have many times ran all day long without being hurt by it, but I have suffered a great deal from hunger, for this is a poor game country."

Wheeler asked if he knew any other White men besides Enoch Fruit who had been mixed up with the Indians. Nampuh replied that there had been a man called "Washoe Charley" who had lived with the Indians for a while, and then had stolen all their best horses and ran off to the Whites again.

Nampuh told about assisting in the killing of a man named Jordan. This Jordan helped kill Indian children and squaws because other Indians had stolen his horses. He said that Jordan was a very bad man, but he was a good fighter.

Nampuh's voice here failed him and he fell back saying, "Everything is getting dark," and lay silent for a while, then spoke in husky, rapid tones, "Look, look, the soldiers are after me. I must go, quick, quick." He then straightened out, and died without a struggle.

Wheeler and Anderson stood and gazed at the dead body for a moment in silence. Two hours before, this gigantic chief had struck terror in Anderson's heart, and now he lay lifeless and harmless, all covered with blood, and the ground all around him saturated by the red tide.

Wheeler turned to Anderson and talked about the death of Nampuh as though nothing unusual had happened. Wheeler remarked that the Indian must be 31 years old, though he looked much older.

Anderson asked, "What should we do next?"

He said, "We will first break their guns to pieces, unless you want one of them."

Anderson responded, "The guns would be useless to me. I am a poor shot."

"In order that the old medicine man may not be made out a liar, I will break them over this rock."

Wheeler collected the big Indian's gun and the other fallen Indian's weapon, and took them to the large rock that Nampuh had hidden behind. He held the barrel of the Mississippi Yager and swung hard against the rock. It took three strong strokes to break the breach and stock and to render the gun useless. He destroyed the second gun against the rock in the same way.

Bill Anderson went along the creek, and with his rope collected his two horses. He came back to where Nampuh lay, put the rope around his feet and with the horse pulled the dead Indian's body 150 yards to the creek. Wheeler then placed the broken gun beside the body. Both men placed brush and rocks over the body, leaving the other Indian in the open where he had fallen.

Anderson returned to his wagon and hitched the horses. Wheeler hopped up beside him and shared the remainder of his lunch. At this point Wheeler turned and spoke.

"Anderson, I want you to not say a word to anyone about what happened today. You understand? If I find out my promise was broken, I will take it up personally with you."

Bill Anderson understood exactly what Wheeler meant.

"I will keep it to myself."

Wheeler hopped down from the wagon and began walking to where his horse was tied. Anderson watched as he walked away, thinking this was the last thing he expected to happen today. Wheeler walked calmly, carrying his rifle in his left hand.

Silver City

A few days later, Anderson saw John Wheeler in Boise. He was very neatly dressed, sitting and conversing quietly with some gentlemen. He did not appear at all like the gunfighter who had, three days before, met and killed in fair combat two of the most desperate of all the braves of Idaho. Anderson wondered if there was more to the story than he knew. What was Wheeler really doing out at Massacre Flats. Was he looking to kill Nampuh and collect the reward? Was the stage coming by just a coincidence? Odd that he had compassion on such a vicious criminal. This deed, which would have been proudly boasted of by almost any other, was kept secret from the world by this singular man.[1]

---

[1] Adapted from a December 1928 account of the killing of Nampuh by William T. Anderson that appeared in the Idaho Statesman.

NINE

Mary Mahoney stepped from the stage and went into the Idaho Hotel. The twenty-one year old Irish woman was traveling from New York to teach school in the West, arriving two days earlier than planned.

She entered the hotel and asked for a room at the front desk. Mary held her head high and had no trace of an Irish accent. Her parents had come from Ireland, but she and a younger sister were born in New York. Both received their education at a private Catholic girl's school. If all went well, her younger sister Kate would follow her West.

The stagehand brought her two traveling bags into the hotel and the clerk handed her a key to a room on the second floor at the rear. She went to the room and, removing her beige bonnet, she sat in the chair, slumping from fatigue. What a long trip to the Owyhees it had been! She took off her clothes except for undergarments and slipped into bed, quickly falling asleep.

Late the following morning, Mary Mahoney woke and lay on her back looking at the ceiling. She felt her heart begin to beat faster along with her breathing. There was just a little rush of excitement in her stomach. She had dreamed and read about the West, and now it belonged to her. This was her adventure.

She sat on the side of the bed and brushed her brown hair back from her blue eyes. She washed in the basin and went down the hall to the newly installed indoor toilet. Returning to the room, she went to the window, and looked over the hillside of homes, and the walled corral and stable behind the hotel. From her castle view the corral looked like an enclosed garden.

She watched a man on a black horse talking with a man at the corral. The man on the horse took off his hat, and she thought she caught a glint of gold, or maybe it was just her imagination. He looked handsome and confident on the black horse. Mary felt a slight knot in her stomach. She shook her head, bringing herself back to the moment, and then dressed, thinking through what needed to be taken care of.

First of all she needed to contact Mr. Reinhart about boarding, and about teaching the local children of Fairview in his boarding house.

****

At seven forty-five in the morning Mary Mahoney rang the bell for the Fairview School. She was the town's new teacher, and she felt excited and pleased that the citizens of the area had selected her. This was actually her second year teaching the children of Fairview. Late last year the town approved the money to build the new schoolhouse. However, the schoolhouse was not finished till the first part of December.

Now, in 1875, she was beginning her first full year in a real schoolhouse. The area around Silver City had grown to a population of around ten thousand people. The children needed teachers and a schoolhouse.

The mining camp on the other side of Silver City and War Eagle Mountain had grown so quickly and to such civilized size that the Owyhee county seat voted funds for a school and teacher. The previous year she had taught the children of Fairview in the boarding house. The citizens of the school district were much impressed with Mary's composure and skills.

Mary looked out over the Snake River plain from the front porch of the school. The view was breathtaking. She watched the children coming down the road from the cluster of homes and businesses nestled into the mountainside. This school for the miner's children was in need of very little. The rich mines in particular, the Golden Chariot in Fairview made for a county which could afford anything a teacher required.

The Fairview School was not as large as the Silver City School. Sixty-three students of varying grades and ages attended the school. She called the children to school with a handbell. They were already wearing winter coats, and, beneath their coats, girls wore black ribbed stockings, wool dresses and white aprons. She could see The Beginner's Reader under their arms.

"Hurry, children!" Mary called, and then turned to enter her schoolroom.

It was early fall and the mornings were cold, and most of the leaves were off the trees. She went to the wood-stove and put more wood into the heat chamber. Then she heard a loud pop. The ice in the wooden water bucket was thawing and the dipper for drinking water hung from the edge of the bucket. Mary went to her desk and reviewed the schoolwork to be covered for the day.

The children entered the school, hung their coats up on the hooks above the wainscoting and went to their desks. Once at their desks they began fussing with the inkwells and preparing their pens. Mary calmed them down, stopping the chatter.

Mary spoke firmly. "Quiet, please! Children, quiet!"

All heads turned toward Mary at the front of the class. She made the perfect picture of a teacher with her gray dress and her high collar wrapped with a band of lace. The school door opened as a young boy of ten came in late, hurrying to hang his coat and find a place to sit. Mary did not draw attention to the boy's tardiness, but waited for him to be seated before she began the day's lesson.

Recess came, and the children went outside. Those who needed to, used the outhouse. In the winter, the games changed from leapfrog, marbles and duck-on-a-rock to coasting and skiing down the slope beside the schoolhouse. At times the snow could be ten feet deep, and the childrens' shoes squeaked when they walked over the compacted snow. Mary saw them as rough diamonds to be polished and burnished into sharp and moral beings. Along with educating them, Mary wished to be an example to them, imparting worthwhile values.

Mary Mahoney lived in Fairview, renting a room at L. B. Reinhart's large two-story lodging house. Her life was simple and fulfilling. On occasion the principal from Silver City would come calling at the school. Oliver Purdy had a solid reputation with the residents of the area, and was part of the original band of men who found gold in Jordan Creek in 1863. He started the first school, and was responsible for keeping the history of the area. When he did call at the Fairview School, Oliver always brought flowers for the room. He would stand stroking his beard and watch sternly as Mary conducted her classes. After he left, some of the older girls would make comments that Mr. Purdy looked more interested in Miss Mahoney than in the quality of education. The older boys did not miss this. They never said anything, but their faces betrayed their thoughts.

When she walked, by the citizens - both rough and civilized – she was greeted with courtesy and respect. In the evenings, she enjoyed her privacy and leisure reading. Mary appeared quite comfortable with her life.

On October 16, 1875, Mary read late into the evening and then retired as normal. The weather had turned cold and there was snow on the ground. She blew out the coal oil lamp and went to sleep.

"Fire, Fire!" Mary heard shouting and pounding on her door. She came awake and wondered if it were a dream. A rose glow filled the room, and there was the smell of smoke. Mary jumped out of bed and went to the window.

"My God!" She looked out, and the entire town was engulfed in flames. She put her slippers and robe on, wrapped her long brown hair up and pinned it, and was out of her room heading for the stair. The rooming house was burning, but flames had not surrounded the entire home. Mary made her way out the front door and then joined the crowd running toward the end of Main Street, where there seemed to be nothing burning.

Fire raged on both sides of the steep slope of Fairview. Mary made it to the end of town and out of reach of the flames. She looked back up the street and watched as men vainly tried to fight the fire. From where she stood, she could see that all was lost. One of the miners standing beside Mary told her that the fire started in Peter Owen's saloon. By now fire had spread to every building. Mary watched as Marcus Moses's tailor shop and the Miner's Union Hall glowed red in the early morning hours. The small enclave of Chinatown was already gutted and collapsing upon itself, sending hot embers into the evening air. Mary thought of her precious school. She could not see it, but she knew it was gone. The school, and all her possessions, lost in the fire! Her cheeks turned pink from the heat, and her eyes were sad. She prayed that no lives were lost.

****

Jacob Deary extended his legs in the stirrups and stood up. He arched his back and stretched every muscle. His entire body ached from riding, and from the work done over the last three days. The black horse stood silent with head down. Jacob had worked on building an earthen dam to hold water during the hot summer months. The job was completed, and he felt secure that the range cattle would have enough water to carry them through till fall.

He and the black horse started the slow walk toward home and the evening meal. Jacob smiled, wondering what Ah Fry was cooking up. The Chinese man had somehow become a real part of J.C.'s and his life. The quiet wily man had a different sense of humor. Ah's white hair, mustache, and long queue gave the aging man a distinguished look.

****

Ah Fry arrived in San Francisco in August of 1852. He left his civilized world and came to the "land of the barbarians". American was in need of cheap labor to build the railroad, to clear the land for farming, and to mine the rich ore. The Chinese immigrants filled the bill, and Ah Fry came for the $30 a month wages.

They were recruited by the thousands through handbills and posters. The head of each household would determine which family members were to leave for America. Ah Fry was chosen by his family. He paid the $54 passage and came to work and to send money home.

He was greeted in San Francisco by representatives of the Tongs, and taken to Little China. From there, Ah Fry was sent to the Sierras to work for the Central Pacific Railroad. The work was back-breaking and dangerous. At news of the gold strike, Ah Fry packed his things and traveled on foot North to Idaho.

The trip was long and hard. However, he fared better than many of his countrymen. Indians found the Chinese easy targets and in particular liked their long braided queues. Indians came upon one hundred or more Chinese traveling to Idaho. The Chief requested they put down their arms, telling them he would not hurt them. When they complied he slaughtered them all, except one boy. The Chief, Egan, even stopped his braves from shooting the foreigners, giving orders that they be beaten to death in order to save ammunition. The renegades scalped them all, and hung their queues on their belts for decoration.

Ah Fry arrived in Silver City, wearing his native dress: a loose shirt and pants, sandals and a cap. He first found work at the War Eagle Hotel as a general laborer, helping with the laundry and with the upkeep of the facility. Later he came to be a cook at the hotel.

Ah Fry endeared himself to the owner, Valentine Blackinger, when he provided helpful suggestions on the use of tea for the Tea Party. Mr. Blackinger gave a party to raise money to pay the debts of St Andrew's Church. He charged $5 a plate. The tea provided by Ah Fry was savory and refreshing to the teetotalers, and The Tea Party was a success.

His needs were simple. Ah Fry ate rice and pork, drank tea, and on special occasions, bought ginger candy. In the back of the Joss House, he lived rent-free in exchange for the upkeep of the house. He saved some money, and sent the rest home to his relatives. His only vice was gambling, and he limited this to once yearly, on the Chinese New Year.

Ah Fry stayed within the Chinese community and went about his business. Silver City was growing and many of its Chinese residents opened businesses or restaurants. Some grew vegetables for the local market, and others worked for themselves, delivering water to homes. Chinese businessmen ran stores selling exotic silks, fans and spices. Opium was sold over the counter in some of them. Others bought the rights to expired claims and reworked the tailings. Several within the Chinese community were able to find profit with the leftovers.

Americans found various ways to taunt the Chinese. Children dug holes along the route of the water carriers, then covered the holes so they could not be detected. When the Chinese water carrier walked over it he would fall in, to the laughter of the children. Some cowboys played rough with foreigners and killed them. The Chinese paid money to the Tongs each month for protection; however, the protection they provided was limited.

During the New Year in February, Ah Fry would find an opium den and play Jaw-bone. He would continue playing until the ceremonies at the Joss House started; then he would pay his respects, helping to light the firecrackers to scare away the evil spirits. This was one of the few times he drank whiskey.

Chinese funerals were an adventure for all in Silver City. Drinking and eating preceded the burial and a grand procession was formed with women mourners, an Oriental band, and a gaily decorated casket riding in a hearse. The remains were taken up Slaughter House Gulch for burial. At the grave, large quantities of food were left for the spirits to eat. Eventually, the remains were packed up and sent back to China for a proper burial.

Jacob knew very little about the Chinese. He never had any trouble with any of them, or did he think of them at all. The ones he had contact with were polite, and they stayed to themselves. He walked up Second Street and came to an unassuming house. There was nothing particularly religious-looking about it. All Jacob knew was that it was a place of worship for the Chinese.

He stepped up on the porch to knock on the door. Jacob paused a moment, noticing all the ornate carving on the door - little panels with intricate forms. They were difficult to see from the street. You had to be right in front of the door to see them.

Jacob knocked and then waited. No reply. Jacob knocked again, except louder. He waited: no reply. He raised his hand to knock again, and a man opened the door.

"Excuse me, I am looking for Ah Fry."

"I am Ah Fry."

"John the Blacksmith said you might be interested in rounding up some mustangs?"

"Could be."

"J. C. McLafferty and myself are looking for a third man to help us round up a herd of mustangs I found. We will split the money three ways. My guess is that there are about a hundred horses and we have about a month of breaking them."

"When you start?"

"Three days from now."

"I will go."

"Good. Meet you at Beachy's stable in three days - six in the mornin'."

Jacob turned to leave, stopped and turned back. "You know anything about horses?"

"No."

Jacob turned and walked away, wondering if John could be mistaken.

Ah Fry closed the door and looked at the drawings of the Joss Gods hanging on the wall. He thanked them for this opportunity. He would work the following day, and then tell his employer he was leaving for a month and would be back. He was certain Mr. Blackinger would honor his request.

****

Jacob and J.C. had worked the ranch for ten years, saved their money, and had avoided trouble with the bank failures. Even though the market for cattle had dropped off locally, the new rail line from Murphy allowed them to ship their cattle and mustangs East. The market for the little mustangs was still good. All in all they were making money.

Jacob thought the black horse would need to be fed and cleaned up, but after that it was time for dinner and to go to bed. He came over the rise and could see the handsome homestead J.C. and he had built. Smoke was coming from the chimney, and Ah Fry was busy preparing the evening dinner. As Jacob came closer to the basalt rock home, he could see another horse in front tied to the rail. He thought it odd that they would have a visitor.

Jacob took the black horse to the barn and removed the saddle. The horse moved from leg to leg in relief of the end of the workday. He took the oat sack down, placing some oats in it, and putting the bag on the horse's head. The horse ate with vigor. Jacob rubbed the horse down as it ate the oats. When it was finished Jacob let the black horse into the corral, and loaded the feed trough with hay.

Jacob stepped up onto the porch and then walked through the door. "Evening, fellas."

"Evening." The men at the table replied in unison. They appeared serious with whatever they were discussing. Jacob went to the stove and poured a cup of coffee and then went to his chair at the table. The place settings were at the table, but Ah Fry had not served dinner yet.

"What's all the fuss?" asked Jacob.

Mike Rohan looked tall even sitting down. He had a long waist, narrow shoulders and a nose that belonged on a hawk. His tan hat was pulled back on his head, he smoked a pipe, and he spoke in a low baritone voice.

"As I was tell'n' J.C., the Indians are raising hell south of here. They have killed some settlers and they're headed for Silver City - or at least in our direction. By the reports we've received, there are about a hundred. We're gathering up some volunteers to head them off. The volunteers are leaving out of Silver City and heading south towards South Mountain. Our best guess is that we'll catch the Indians there.

"I came to get you boys to join up to help fight the Indians."

J.C. answered immediately. "We're in." Jacob nodded in agreement.

"What we need you men to do is ride to O'Keefe's Ranch. Sorry, but you need to be there by first light. You'll need to ride most of the night."

"We'll be there." J.C. replied.

"I knew we could count on ya. I need to ride to a couple of more ranches before tomorrow morning, so I need to leave. See you men in the morning."

Mike left, and J.C. and Jacob went to the stove and fixed a helping of food. They ate quickly and grabbed some jerky for the trip. Jacob took his Springfield rifle down from the wall and put it in the scabbard to carry on the black horse. They were going into battle.

****

The dapple-gray mare leaned back and then lunged forward three quick times to clear the steep bank of the Snake River. Buffalo Horn and his sixty braves crossed the river at Glenns Ferry. On the other side, the Indians cut the ferry loose to slow down any pursuing soldiers.

Captain Reuben F. Bernard had driven Buffalo Horn and his braves from the Camas Prairie. The Indians were outraged that permission was given for the Whites to settle the prairie. The settlers moved in to the valued land, permitting their hogs and cattle to eat the camas plants. The Indians relied on the camas plant for food during the summer, and they were already struggling to eat and keep from starving. The Indians had nowhere else to go.

Lines of strain on the face of Buffalo Horn showed his anger and worry for his people. He had come from helping the Whites in the north as a scout only to be betrayed when he returned home. What made the Indian hostilities even sadder was that the war was caused by a bureaucrat's error in reserving "Kansas Prairie" rather than "Camas Prairie". The recalcitrant officials refused to correct the error, and the settlers were allowed to settle the Camas Prairie Reservation of Buffalo Horn.

The braves gathered together before moving toward South Mountain. They had attacked freight wagons, and resupplied their ammunition. Any Whites to get in their way were to die. Buffalo Horn sent the women and children by another route into the Eastern Oregon Territory. The only salvation the settlers of the Bruneau Valley had was that a friendly Indian, by the name of Bruneau John, warned many settlers before Buffalo Horn arrived. The settlers left their farms and went to the nearby caves for safety. Once in the Oregon Territory, Buffalo Horn planned to meet with other

Silver City

Indian tribes and launch an all-out war on the invading Whites.

The band of Indians began moving through the Owyhees. Captain Bernard was on the trail of Buffalo Horn. The Indians made a bivouac a few miles from the small mining town of South Mountain. During the encampment, Buffalo Horn and his council went to pay their respects to a White friend, Pete Disenroff, who ranched close to South Mountain. Pete had hired many of the Bannocks to help bring in the hay, and he treated the Indians with respect. Buffalo Horn and his council were having dinner with Pete when an Indian scout interrupted the dinner to inform the chiefs about the volunteers from Silver City camped at O'Keefe's Ranch. Buffalo Horn and his braves left the dinner and went to prepare for battle.

****

Jacob and J.C. rode quietly down the mountainside to the O'Keefe Ranch. They could see the outline of the home, the outbuildings and the corral. The false light of morning gave detail to the encampment of men from Silver City.

"Who goes there?"

Jacob replied, "Volunteers, Jacob Deary and J.C. McLafferty."

"Good to have ya. There should be grub in the house." replied the fellow volunteer.

The two men dismounted and tied their horses to the rail by the water trough. They both were bone tired and walked slowly to the house, pushing back the door and walking in. Inside, a dozen men were sleeping on the floor, and Mrs. O'Keefe stood by the hot stove with coffee ready.

In a quiet voice she spoke, "Mornin'."

Jacob and J. C. each took a cup of coffee and a biscuit. The men sleeping on the floor were beginning to wake up and more were stirring outside. Within a half hour most of the volunteers were up and getting their gear and horses ready to move out.

They walked out of the home and to the corral where the other men were gathered. The morning light was replaced with the first rays of sun. By the corral stood Captain J.B. Harper. He brought the volunteers from Silver City and acted as the leader. Beside him stood two Indians. J.B. Harper spoke in a firm voice to the men.

"We will move out shortly. I will take the lead and our scouts will be with me. You men know the signals, so stay alert. We believe the savages are headed for the Oregon Territory and will cut through on South Mountain. Just where, I am not sure. We will proceed toward the mining town."

The men were quiet and somber. The conflict with the Indians had become real, and not a boasting match.

"You men have any questions?"

Silence followed.

"Good. Prepare to move out."

Jacob and J.C. were at the back of the crowd. Jacob caught a look at the Indians, but not quite well enough to see them completely. There was something familiar about one of them.

The men mounted their horses and set out in a double column behind the Captain and two Indian scouts.

Close to noon the column moved along the north side of South Mountain. The volunteers stayed to the center of the valley and in the open to avoid a direct ambush. The sun was hot, and the horses need to be watered. Ahead and to the right was an open area with running water. Suddenly, the two Indians at the front of the column froze. The Captain kept riding for a moment and then stopped and turned back to see what had happened. Captain Harper could see the urgency in their faces. He reigned his horse back to face the column and gave the signal to stop.

Exploding out of the tree line came the ear-deafening sound of rifle fire and the hooves of sixty horses. Buffalo Horn and his braves had lain in ambush for the volunteers and had picked the best ground for attack. The soldiers looked up to the Indians driving down on them. Their horses shied and moved sideways and were startled by the gunfire and noise. The volunteers, working to keep their horses in check were unable to reach their rifles. Those from the front of the column were barely keeping their horses under control, and they fell back into the middle of the column, further confusing the men and horses. Several volunteers pulled their handguns to return the fire. The Indians were coming closer and all the men from Silver City could see they were overpowered. The volunteers began to panic.

Jacob brought his black stallion under control and reached for his pistol. His horse jumped and swayed with the excitement and it took longer than he wanted before he brought an attacking Indian into his sights. He fired, watching the Indian fall backwards over his horse. Shortly they would be overrun and would be fighting hand-to-hand and outnumbered. It was time to retreat. He looked as a number of horses reared back on their hind legs. Two of the riders were off their horses, on the ground, and working to regain their feet and fire their pistols. Jacob knew they were lost.

Jacob felt another volunteer's horse hit the side of his, and he looked to the right. He froze as he looked directly into the eyes of the scout Paiute Joe. He saw the gold key he had left in the cave on a leather lace around the Indian's neck. Paiute Joe looked at Jacob - with surprise, smiled, then regained control of his horse and pulled away. Jacob was shocked, and for a moment - the past pressed up against him. Suddenly he felt a stinging in his right thigh and looked down to see where an Indian had grazed his leg with a knife. Jacob swung the Colt to the right and fired directly into the Indian's head. From the side he could see the volunteers retreating down hill. Jacob looked up, saw Paiute Joe with his Enfield rifle extended, and heard the deafening concussion. He followed the barrel to see the target. At less than twenty yards was Chief Buffalo Horn. Paiute Joe sent the lead ball directly to the heart of the Indian Chief. The slug picked the Chief off his horse and threw him over its back and to the ground. The body of Buffalo Horn lay lifeless on the earth.

As though a rip through eternity had pierced the battleground, the braves under Buffalo Horn knew instantly that their Chief was dead. Their anger and aggression were transformed into a collective grief, and they stopped their pursuit of the volunteers. The volunteers from Silver City fled out of reach of the Indians, collecting themselves in the valley. They knew that if the Chief had not been shot, they all would be dead. The Indians gathered their Chief and left without further assault, disappearing into the tree line.

The volunteers mounted their horses and returned to the battlefield. Two horses stood without riders. The men collected the bodies of Chris Steuder and Oliver Purdy. They wrapped the bodies in tarps and tied them over the saddles of their horses. The column formed again and began the silent trek back to Silver City. Captain Harper led the volunteers home. Before reaching the O'Keefe ranch, Paiute Joe and his brother separated from the column and headed out toward the West.

Jacob rode slowly and silently within the column of volunteers. He felt the sting of the thigh wound. The death of the two volunteers seemed to underscore the losses he had experienced over the last thirteen years. Jacob's grief went to his gut and stayed until he reached Silver City.

TEN

Snow was piled eight feet high in the streets of Silver City. Patrons had difficulty getting into the Idaho Hotel. All along the streets cold and snow made life hard. Jacob Deary sat at the breakfast table reading an article in the newspaper "The Avalanche". This was the second time he read through it. He took a sip of coffee, leaned back and savored the article.

December 10, 1878

> "BALL AT WAGONTOWN: Supplied with one of Tim Regan's best turnouts we bundled up Mrs. <u>Avalanche</u>, shook the snow of Silver City off our feet, and attended the ball given by that prince among good fellows, Tom Walls, at Wagontown, night before last. The ball was given to honor our brave volunteers who pushed the Indian threat away from our door."

> "We arrived at the festive scene about four o'clock in the afternoon and found a numerous delegation already present from Silver City and Jordan Valley. They still kept coming and by dark the extensive stables were crowded full of equines munching hay and grain, and the premises all about the

establishment were crowded with sleighs of every description, from the family outfit capable of containing a dozen persons to a dry goods box on runners just big enough to hold the average country swain and his sweetheart."

"By six o'clock the ladies had completed their toilets, and the volunteers donned clean colors and adjusted their neckties. Tom Walls then gave the word of command and the gay throng filled the large dining room where ample justice was done to an excellent dinner prepared for the occasion, the appetites of the many of the company being sharpened by a sleigh-ride of twenty and even thirty miles."

"Immediately after dinner the premises were cleared for action. The dancing hall upstairs was brilliantly lighted for the occasion, and across one end was stretched a large American Flag, which warmed up the patriotic feelings of the company as befits this honorable occasion. Ben Butler, of Jordan Valley, was Master of Ceremonies and performed the arduous duties incumbent upon him in the most satisfactory manner to all present."

"Ben Butler introduced the Territorial Governor of Idaho, John P. Hoyt. The Honorable Governor praised the Silver City Volunteers. Governor Hoyt honored Chris Steuder and O. H. Purdy who lost their lives in the battle with the Bannocks. In particular, The Governor praised O. H. Purdy for his bravery and for being the volunteer who shot Buffalo Horn and ended the conflict. Without O. H. Purdy's bravery more lives would have been lost."

"The Names of the men who participated in the fight against the Indians are J. E. Harper, O. H. Purdy, Chris. Steuder, Tom Jones, Guy Newcomb, Frank Martin, Ole Anderson, John Davidson, Ben White, Wm. Nichols, P. Donnelly, Mark Leonard, John Posey, W. Cooper, Geo Graham, J. M. Brunzell, John Anderson, Nick Maher, Wm. Manning, W. W. Hastings, Al Myers, M. M. Rogers, Joe Rupert, J. J. Outhouse, J. M. Dillenger, Alex Wellman, Frank Armstrong, Paiute Joe and his brother. The following are the names of the volunteers who left here on Saturday and Sunday: W. H. Angell, Billy Williams, A. J. Palmer, Geo. W. Palmer, Con Shea, D. Driscoll, R. Z. Johnson, Tim Shea, Dave Shea, John Catlow, Charles Miller, C. Sprowls, L. McIntyre, J. Laure, Joe Oldham, Lark Richardson, Joe Brown, E. Mills, J. W. Posey, Tim Regain, Jack McKenzie, John Connors, Mike Rohan, Bronko Bill, J. Gusman, Jacob Deary, J.C. McLafferty, Ben Davis, Jack Stoddard, Charley Hays and several others."

"Before the dancing began Governor John P. Hoyt asked all of the volunteers to stand in the center of the dance floor. He took from the bandstand a box and opened it. To the surprise of all the box contained a golden apple. A local blacksmith formed it and the gold for the apple was donated by the citizens of Silver City."

"Ben Butler then introduced the new teacher for Jordan Valley, Miss Mary Mahoney. The Governor gave the apple to Miss Mahoney and asked her to toss it into the crowd of noble knights who defended Silver City. The volunteer who caught the apple could keep it as a token of appreciation from the citizens. Miss Mahoney took hold of the apple and gallantly threw the orb into the volunteers. The hands went up, but the trophy went to quick Jacob Deary. He is the richer and so are the citizens of Silver City."

"Dancing commenced about 7 o'clock to the merry strains of music from Ralph Goodliffe's Banjo and Luke Crandalls's violin. Each gentleman was designated by a number, by which means none were slighted and all had an opportunity to trip the 'light fantastic' to their heart's content."

"It was a gay party. The beauty and chivalry of Silver City and Jordan Valley were there. Old pioneers whom we have seen dance to the music of the Indian war whoop and bullet ten and eleven years ago, now joined in the lazy waltz and lively quadrille with no fear of losing their scalps. Some of the younger male participants, however, encountered the more pleasing, though not less fatal, danger of losing their hearts - at least we judge so from considerable billing and cooing that we noticed on the sly."

"Some of the ladies present, viz: Mrs. Brainard, Mrs. Ira Corp, Mrs. Clegg, Mrs. Marshall Hill, Miss Annawalt, Miss McCoole, Miss Mary Mahoney, Mrs. Keenan, Mrs. Butler, Mrs. Skinner, Miss Collister, Mrs. Bradley, Mrs. W. J. Hill, Miss Mary O'Keefe, Mrs. Mills, and Miss Lizzie Connors, besides the sprightly and amiable hostess, Mrs. Walls."

"Dancing continued without intermission till midnight, when the merry company again repaired to the dining room and partook of a magnificent supper, such a one as Tom Walls and his amiable help-mate are famous for spreading before their guests."

"At one o'clock dancing was resumed under the management of a committee of ladies, who were determined to assert and avail themselves of the privilege accorded to them one year out of four, and from that time forward, the word of command, also given by fair lips was 'ladies take your partners for the next dance,' thus reversing the role of the former part of the night."

"Dancing was kept up till long after daylight—between seven and eight o'clock—in the morning, when the jolly party sat down to a splendid breakfast, which they partook of with zest after the well-earned gayeties of night. Then, teams were hitched up, goodbyes were said, and the happy, but sleepy crowd took their departure for their respective homes. Altogether it was one of the jolliest and most pleasant social parties that we ever attended, and we felt that it was good to be there. Aside from the pleasure and enjoyment incident to such an occasion, it afforded us an opportunity to meet and converse with our friends, so many of whom, with their wives, daughters and sweethearts we never saw together before."

"We believe that the jolly folks of Jordan Valley are the most persevering dancers in the world - too much for us in Silver City."

Jacob leaned back in his chair and took another sip of coffee. The memories of the previous night were just great. He had never danced before, but somehow she made it easy and he thoroughly enjoyed the adventure. She was lean and what a lovely smile, and best of all, she was Irish.

****

Mary sat nervously at the end of the hall with the dignitaries. She was chosen to throw the golden apple to the volunteers. How she had been chosen she did

Silver City

not know. This was an honor. Governor Hoyt said a few words and then motioned her to stand and come to him. The Governor opened the box and removed the lovely hand-crafted golden apple. She turned and looked out over the crowd.

Those who were guests and not volunteers moved to the side of the room and only the Indian fighters were left in the center of the room.

Toward the back of the crowd of volunteers she saw the young man she had noted before. Her heart skipped a beat when she saw the tan face and sculpted features of the man. He wore a white shirt and looked strong and healthy. She knew the golden apple was meant for him. Mary Mahoney took the apple into her hand and the sounds of the room faded away. With a long graceful underhand toss, she threw the apple into an arch, which seemed frozen in air. The apple went to the back of the volunteers and landed in the hand of Jacob Deary. Her heart sang with joy. A loud roar went up from all and a handshake all around for Jacob. He went to Mary to say hello and she moved toward him to congratulate him.

Jacob smiled and said, "Guess I'm lucky."

"Yes, I think you are. Would you like to dance?"

Jacob's face flushed at the prospect. He replied "Yes, I'm not real sure about it."

Graciously, she responded, "We will learn together."

Mary placed her hand on Jacob's shoulder and they began to move along the dance floor. First awkwardly, then with each step more gracefully. Then they began to dance as one. She could feel the strength in his shoulder. She was captivated.

****

"How much money you got?"

J.C. looked back over his shoulder while filing the shoe on the horse.

"What?"

Jacob repeated the question. "How much money you got?"

J.C. put down the leg of the horse and turned back to Jacob, tilted his head, squinted one eye and asked, "What's go'n' on?"

"Three Forks is up for bid from the government." Jacob replied.

"That's a nice chunk of property."

"That's right, and I figure we have as good a chance to win the bid as anyone else. Con Shea has more than his hands full with the property he has, so that leaves us as the likely high bidders. You throw your money in with mine and we'll get the property. How's it sound?" Jacob continued, "As I remember the place, there is a spring that runs year round from Soldier Creek and there is still a stand of pine trees we can use for lumber. The Juniper trees we can use for fence posts. That property is tucked away against the mountain, and it's protected from the snows and wind. The main property is flat, and the old army buildings can be converted for housing and outbuilding. I'll live there and run the property and you live here and run this property. We'll split the profits on the stock we raise. Sound about right?"

J.C. answered, "I'm in."

The two ranchers rode to the Silver City courthouse. Inside, they presented their envelope containing the bid to the county recorder for the old

Camp Three Forks. The two men waited the month for the opening of the bids. Jacob had rebuilt the property in his mind and appeared preoccupied as he worked. J.C. watched in amused silence.

The month passed slowly, but the day came for the opening of the bids. They rode to Silver City and again entered the courthouse, where there stood a cluster of other ranchers who had placed bids, or who were there out of curiosity. Con Shea was in the courthouse, which worried both J.C. and Jacob. Finally, the clerk came from the back room with the sheriff.

The bald-headed man with spectacles held the envelope with the winning bid. He removed the paper with the name of the high bidder for the abandoned army camp.

"The highest bid, and thus the property, belongs to Deary and McLafferty. They are the owners of the Camp Three Forks property. Money is to be brought to this office by three o'clock today to complete the transaction."

J.C. and Jacob rode back to their ranch west of Silver City. They rode at an easy pace, savoring the future and talking of the changes the purchase of Camp Three Forks would make in their lives. This meant that they were partners in a large enterprise, and not just surviving.

Out of the quiet Jacob spoke, "I'd like to take Ah Fry for my cook."

J.C. turned sideways and said, "Fine by me. All he wants to do with me is argue."

****

Ah Fry drove the loaded buckboard and Jacob rode his black stallion alongside. The sky was clear but the road to Three Forks was muddy from the previous day's rain. They turned up the side road leading to the abandoned Camp Three Forks along Soldier Creek. As they worked their way along the rutted road, they passed a barn, built by the soldiers to shelter livestock, on the lower end of the creek. Jacob and Ah Fry came up on the main camp, and Ah Fry reined the horses to a stop. Jacob looked over the buildings. All the structures were built with large pine longs from further up Soldier Creek. They were strong and solid, even though they had been abandoned and were in disrepair.

The officers' house was a one-story structure with individual rooms and one large room for meals. The enlisted men had been housed in one large, long log structure with bunks side by side, and the third structure was the utility building that housed the washrooms and repair shops. Looking across the creek Jacob saw where cellars had been dug into the side of the mountain for the keeping of ammunition or food stores. There was a smaller corral by the creek where the cavalry mounts were kept. Jacob knew he would need to fence a much larger area.

Ah Fry began to unload the supplies and tools for the work of rebuilding the camp into a living, working ranch complex. Jacob felt the tidal wave of work that needed to be done and was deciding just where to start. He walked through and inspected the buildings to see which would become his home, and possibly that of his future wife.

The weeks passed and they were into the hot, dry time of August. Jacob worked at stringing fence line. Ah Fry's duties were to get the living quarters in shape for them and for any hired hands. Jacob used the gnarly Juniper trees for fence posts. Juniper was plentiful, but hard to work with. Jacob set the green fence posts and then strung the barbed wire, building thirty miles of fence line. The cattle would be grazing on open range and would be brought in prior to being sold. He could keep his horses and mules within the corral close to the ranch, and use the stock shed at the end of the property to protect the animals during hot sun or snow.

The day came when the house and property were once more in good repair. Jacob took the tools back to the tool shed, mounted his black stallion and rode the seventeen miles to Three Forks Canyon—where the East, West, and North Forks of the Owyhee rivers converge. He aimed to treat himself right and take a long soak in the natural hot water pools along the river.

Jacob rode slowly and without concern for time. He intended this as an escape from work. At the rim of the canyon he looked down. What a sight! The high canyon walls converged and encased the three rivers. On the far side he could see where the soldiers had tried to build a road over the canyon and onto the flat land. The road zigzagged up the incline only to end toward the top. The rock had been so hard and difficult to cut through that the soldiers gave up. Soldiers had lived in the large cave in the canyon wall.

He gently put a heel into the flank of his horse and began the descent into the canyon. The wagon road was steep and narrow with several switchbacks on the way down. He reached the bottom, and where the three rivers converged he dismounted and watered his horse. The horse grazed on the grass close to the creek for a while, then Jacob mounted again and walked his horse up the main fork of the Owyhee River. The river was low in August and the riverbed solid. He rode on till he saw steam rising out of the bank on the north side of the river.

Jacob removed the saddle from the black horse and hobbled it along the river edge. He took off his boots and walked across the river. The water in the river was warm from the run-off from the hot springs. He climbed the rock face and reached a level outcropping. He was standing on the edge of a deep, hot pool.

He stacked his clothes in a pile close to the pool and stood naked in the sunlight. He eased down into the hot water brought up from deep within the earth. The pool was chest deep and he stood easily in it. He leaned back to where the water flowed from above and into the pool. The water flowed over his shoulders and pounded all the soreness out of his aching muscles. He looked out to the far canyon wall that shot straight up. The soldiers from Camp Three Forks had come here to relax and Indians for centuries had come also. Now, this country belonged to him - at least for today.

Jacob thought about J.C. and how both the properties could be split with each having their ranch independent of each other. Jacob could raise horses and J.C. could raise cattle - each on his own ranch. Jacob turned his head sideways and there on the edge of the hot springs sat a coyote, looking at him. Jacob looked directly into the coyote's eyes and he could have sworn the coyote read his mind and knew his soul. Then the animal stood up and slowly walked away.

****

Mary Mahoney placed the textbooks on the edge of her desk, straightened it, and looked out over the schoolroom. All is in order, she thought. The day and week were done and the new school year should develop into a challenge. She enjoyed teaching in Jordan Valley and had taught the children of the growing community since the fire in Fairview. Mary was no stranger to the area. She walked to the coat rack and removed her light fall coat and put it on. The door of the schoolroom opened and there stood Jacob Deary. The last thing she expected at the end of this day was to have this man walk into her school.

Jacob held his hat in his hand. "Good afternoon."

Mary returned the smile. "Come in. A pleasure to see you."

Jacob was not skilled at small talk, but he tried. "How's school going?"

"Well the children are a challenge, but are doing well. I thoroughly enjoy teaching."

"I came by to see if you would like to get together this Saturday?"

"As a matter of fact, I have no plans. Did you have anything in particular in mind?"

"The horse races are starting in Jordan this week, how about we go on Saturday?"

"Sounds grand. Come by the Joyces' around noon?"

Jacob nodded and said, "See ya Saturday." He turned and walked out of the schoolhouse. Jacob was walking ten feet off the ground.

Mary had hoped to see Jacob Deary again, but had given up, since it had been so long since the dance. Her heart was singing and she could hardly wait till Saturday.

Saturday came, and Jacob Deary pulled up in his buckboard pulled by a matched team of white horses. He wore a white shirt and blue denim pants, and was as ready as any man could be. He climbed down and went to the door of the house. Before he could knock Mary opened the door and stood before him. She looked beautiful. Her dress was light blue and came high on her neck. Her cheeks were rosy and she had a lovely twinkle in her eye.

They walked to the buckboard and Jacob helped Mary into the seat. With one hand he held the small of her back and with the other hand supported her arm as he helped her into the buckboard. He felt the warmth of her body and the lean muscles of her back.

They rode the short distance to the track just out of town. It originally had been swampland, but it was filled in with dirt, making an excellent racing surface. Riders said the track was fast because of the spring of the sod. In fact, the Jordan Valley horse races had turned into a real event. They lasted all week and attracted racing and horse enthusiasts from all over the Northwest. Indian and rancher raced side by side. The races also brought the brothel women from Silver City, and gamblers from miles around.

Jacob and Mary arrived shortly after the races had started, and Jacob put the buckboard and team across the road and out of the way. They walked through the excited crowd and made their way to the makeshift stands. As they came around the side of the stands and began to climb to a better seat, Jacob heard a familiar voice.

"Hello, Jacob!" Lola spoke in a deep lusty voice and gave him a big smile.

Jacob replied in a friendly manner. "Hello, Lola. Enjoying the races?"

"Of course, best business all year."

Mary looked at the painted face and flashy clothes of the woman. In spite of her obvious profession, she was beautiful. Mary chose not to ask Jacob how he knew her.

They found a seat high in the stands where they could easily see each race. They were pushed together like sardines on the bare plank. Prior to the start of each race everyone would stand to have a better view of the horses. The horses jumped off the start line, the crowd would roar, and individuals could be heard cheering for a particular horse. As the horses came closer to the finish line the crowd's collective voice would become louder and after they crossed the finish line, the volume of the voices would drop off and the spectators would sit back down, and waiting for the next race.

The races ended in late afternoon and the citizens returned home and the visitors, to their bedrolls. Jacob and Mary walked back to the buckboard and drove home. He walked her to the door.

"I had a wonderful time, Jacob." Mary beamed at Jacob.

"So did I. How about we get together again?"

"I would love to. Let me make a picnic lunch before the weather turns?"

"I'm willing. In a couple of weeks?"

"Two weeks from Sunday."

"Then Sunday it is. See you in two weeks about noon."

Jacob worked hard over the next two weeks, but his mind kept returning to Mary and his anticipation of seeing her again. Even at night when he was dog-tired he kept thinking of her. He tossed and turned in his sleep. The ranch became more than a place to raise livestock, it was looking like a place to raise a family. His heart would sing when he thought of all the possibilities.

Mary conducted her teaching skills without a flaw, yet there was just the hint of distraction about her. She was attentive to the students' needs, yet she hesitated a fraction of a second when answering their questions. Mary was thinking of the picnic and her next meeting with Jacob.

Two long weeks went by, and Jacob returned to the Joyce residence to meet with Mary and leave for the picnic. At the door they greeted each other, and just inside the doorway was the basket prepared for the picnic. Jacob leaned in and picked it up. It was heavier than he expected. They climbed onto the buckboard and headed north of town along Jordan Creek. The creek meandered north and then turned west just below the rimrock along the edge of the valley. A stand of trees made shade for a beautiful picnic and the green of them contrasted with the black lava formations of the rimrock. The clear stream added the finishing touch.

Jacob brought the buckboard to a halt, climbed down and walked to the other side to help Mary climb out of the buckboard. Her dress was cream colored, almost the color of skin. He went to the back and

Silver City

retrieved the basket. Mary carried two blankets in her arms. They scouted the stream and found a cool and level place. She spread the blankets and began to unpack the food.

"Looks good."

"Mr. Joyce shot some sage hens and I fried them up for the picnic." She smiled and looked at Jacob.
Jacob reached in and pulled out a mason jar with a dark liquid. "What's this?"

"I thought a little wine would be good with our lunch."

Mary laid out the tin plates and took two tin cups and poured half a cup of wine in each. They both were quiet, enjoying the fall day. Warmth from the ground came up through the blanket and the rustling of leaves mixed with the running stream made for a delight of the senses.

"I remember seeing you when I first arrived in Silver City."

"How's that?"

"I was staying at the Idaho Hotel and watched you riding a black horse out back."

"You're right, I did work there - for Hill Beachy." Jacob smiled at the thought she had had her eye on him for a while.

Mary continued to talk as she served the sage hen and salad onto the plates. She passed the plate to Jacob and both stopped talking. Mary poured more wine for both from the jar. They were hungry, and ate the food with gusto. Jacob reached into the basket and pulled out two more pieces of sage hen. When his plate was clean, he leaned back full length on the blanket. He looked up through the trees to the blue of the sky and a scattering of dark clouds. The air was warm and had the fragrance of fall in it. Mary sat eating slowly, straight up, looking poised and comfortable.

Jacob broke the silence first. "You plan to stay in the area?"

Mary spoke from her heart. "I love it here. There is something about the way the light catches the grass in the morning and in the evening and there is a clean blue to the sky. I just love it and there is something else I can't quite put into words. It has to do with how primitive the land is. I am not quite sure. I do plan to stay here."

"Glad to hear it." Jacob felt the same way about the land. Somehow it had captured his soul and this is where he planned to raise a family and be buried.

Jacob felt a change in the air. A short, gentle gust pushed over them and then disappeared as quickly as it had come. He sat up from his half sleep and dreams. Mary sat watching Jacob. He looked up at the sky and saw rapidly moving dark clouds. Again a gust of chilled air washed over them. Then a sudden steady blast. The horses whinnied and Jacob went to the team and tied their harnesses with a rope and the rope to a tree.

The raindrops were gentle at first, then began to increase in intensity. Jacob went back to where Mary was hurrying to collect the picnic gear. A flash of lightning and the delayed loud clap of thunder. Jacob knew the lightning was close.

"Give me that." Jacob motioned with his head for Mary to hand him the basket. She lifted it and he quickly took it from her and began walking toward the rimmrock.

"Quick, this way." He took off at almost a run up the side of the hill through the sagebrush and grass toward a dark opening in the rock. Mary hurried behind Jacob carrying the blankets. The rain began coming down in sheets and the wind drove it sideways. It became difficult to see and the ground was becoming slippery.

"Hurry." Jacob turned and grabbed Mary's hand, making long quick strides up the slope. Then they stood in the opening of a cave in the rimrock. The opening was large enough for both to stand. Once in the cave and out of the rain both realized they were soaked from the sudden downpour. They looked out from the entrance to the heavy sheets of rain, black clouds, and flashes of lightning. Both were breathing hard from the sprint up the hillside. Jacob could see the buckboard and horses below. They were tied securely and staying put.

Jacob leaned close to Mary and put his arm around her shoulder. He could feel the damp and cold coming through her clothes. She was shaking from the cold - a full body tremor.

"You're freezing." Jacob spoke in a deep tone. Mary did not answer.

"Here." Jacob took both of the blankets and began to wrap them around her. He pulled her to his body to bring her warmth. With his arms around her he felt the full pressure of her body. She curled up under his arms and moved close to him for warmth and protection. They stood together for a long moment and until she stopped trembling from the cold. She leaned back and looked up into his eyes and neither could resist the other and they kissed - a long passionate kiss.

"Sit back here out of the wind." Jacob took Mary to the back of the cave. They both sat down and leaned against the cave wall. Again they kissed. She dropped the blankets from her shoulders and put both her arms around his neck.

Outside the rain continued to come down in sheets and the dark angry clouds swiftly moved overhead. For a brief moment the flash of lightning lit the entire area with an otherworld light and soon after came the thunder which shook the earth.

****

Father Toner made the ride from Silver City to Trout Creek. He knew it was God's work, but he felt old and the ride was longer than he remembered. He rode to Lone Tree Creek Ranch, the home of Jacob Deary's new partner Den Driscoll. Father Toner tied his horse to the corral fence. The visitors' horses occupied the hitching rail at the front of the ranch house. He walked onto the porch, then stopped and dusted himself off and made sure his collar was placed properly. In his left hand he held the Bible he intended to use in the marriage ceremony.

Inside the men sat and stood around the table in the kitchen drinking whiskey. Two women hurried and worked feverishly to prepare dinner for the twenty odd people that had come to celebrate the marriage of Jacob Deary and Mary Julia Mahoney. Occasionally, a woman would slap the hand of a man who was attempting to grab a dinner sample. Jacob stood with the men. He appeared relaxed, and held a glass of whiskey in his hand. No one noticed that he did not drink the whiskey. There were two toasts, and he raised the glass to his mouth, but stayed away from the whiskey. He did not want his senses dulled for his marriage. This was a dream come true.

Mary stood in the back bedroom before a dressing mirror. She was excited, anxious, and fearful at the same time.

"How do I look?" Mary asked Kate.

"Dear, you look beautiful. You quit fussing. All the jaws of those old cowboys are going to drop when they get an eyeful of you." Mary's sister Kate had come from Boise for the wedding.

Again Mary looked back at the mirror and saw the full length of the dress. The white satin had been bought in Boise and the dress created by Kate and now, the last-minute fitting was taking place. Kate bent over and placed one more pin in the side, relaxed the back and quickly tucked the seam and stitched it together. Mary's trim waist fit perfectly in the wedding dress.

In one half of the living area the women were making the last minute food preparations and setting the table. The table had maple wood legs, clawed feet, and inlaid pear wood at each corner, burled edges, and a maple zebra pattern on the sides. The table was long, with four leaves, and honey-colored like an old violin. All twenty people would sit at it comfortably. All the lamps were lit and the long dining table gave the room the look of a large European banquet hall.

Father Toner finished his second glass of whiskey with the men. Kate came from the back bedroom to see what was holding up the ceremony. She walked over to Father Toner, placed her fists on her hips, and asked if he was about ready. The tone of her voice let the priest know it was time to begin. He coughed, stood up and walked to the far end of the living room.

Mary entered the room wearing her white satin wedding dress, and all gasped at her beauty. She looked fresh and young, just a little anxious. Her smile was genuine and charming. Jacob stood at the back of the room in his black suit and white shirt. He looked serious and handsome, with his angular features and broad forehead. When Mary entered the room his expression changed from seriousness to one of delight. He kept a slight smile on his face during the entire ceremony.

The two came together at the back of the room and walked arm in arm up to Father Toner. The crowd behind them shared in Jacob's and Mary's joy.

"Friends and guests, we're gathered here to join Jacob Deary and Miss Mary Mahoney in the Sacrament of Matrimony." A white lock of hair hung down from the aging priest's forehead, and he ran his words together just enough to let all know he had a little too much whiskey. During the ceremony, Father Toner would lean back on his heels and all at the ceremony would stop breathing just a moment, because no one was sure he would not fall over.

"Now, I pronounce you man and wife." Father Toner completed the ceremony and the newlyweds turned to each other. Jacob took Mary into his arms and kissed her. The friends and guests gave a loud cheer.

They turned, and the friends gathered round to congratulate the two. They sat down at the table for their wedding feast. Each of the men proposed a toast for the couple, with each trying to outdo the others. All the plates were filled with meat and vegetables, and the pies were on the side cupboard waiting for the main meal to be finished.

The front door of house opened, and they turned with surprise at the interruption. There in the doorway stood the blacksmith, John Forney. However, for this event he was dressed like a king with a new suit, combed and trimmed hair, and a wonderful smile.

"Sorry I am late." John boomed.

"Come in, we are glad you made it! Here, slide that chair over here and set a place for John." Jacob stood up and walked to John, giving him a welcoming handshake. All were pleased that the king of blacksmiths made the wedding.

The feast continued till late afternoon when all said farewell to Jacob and Mary Deary. The newlyweds climbed onto the buckboard and headed for home and their life together at Three Forks Ranch.

****

Mary held a square nail in her hand high up on the log wall of their home. The officers' quarters was being turned into a home for two, and for a baby on the way. She held the fabric tight and stretched it to the ceiling. Now, she needed to secure it with a wood strip and nail. Mary was almost done with covering the dingy log walls with fabric. Jacob walked in and saw her stretching and standing on her toes.

"Here, give me that." He walked over, taking the hammer and nail. Easily he hit the head, driving the nail into the slat and into the log. He held the fabric in place and motioned for Mary to hand him some more nails. She did, and he completed the section of the wall.

"How's it look?" Jacob asked as he stood back eyeing his work.

"Perfect."

"This is turning into a real home. Give us a few more months and we will have the make'n's of a real family." Jacob spoke to Mary with pride.

Mary was eight months pregnant and it showed. She worked hard on the house each day, getting the place ready for the newcomer and for Christmas. Only one week, and the Holiday would be here.

What brought Ah Fry and Mary together as friends was the new Easter Range Jacob bought as a wedding present. He had purchased it a month before the wedding, and it took five months to arrive. Six men had to carry it into the home and set it in place. It was an item that brought prestige to a western woman, as well as luxury and ease.

Ah Fry was equally impressed with the stove. He purchased coal to feed the fire and polished it daily. He worked with it to find just the right temperature for bread, stews, and meats. The Easter Range had delicate lacework patterns all across it and a chrome strip adorned the top and bottom edge. The oven door had the name Easter embossed on it, and to the left on the door of the chink box was the date, 1883.

There was snow on the ground outside and the days and nights were cold. J.C. and he had split up as partners and now Den Driscoll and Jacob were sharing rangeland for their joint horse and sheep enterprises. The mines in Silver City were up and running again after the bank collapse, and, for Jacob Deary, business could not have been better.

Kate Mahoney arrived from Boise to help Mary around the house and with her delivery. The baby would be coming anytime. The women were hoping for a New Year's baby. After Christmas, Kate and Mary were taken to the home of Mrs. Driscoll at Lone Tree Creek Ranch to have the baby. Den Driscoll's wife was a midwife and would assist with the delivery.

Then, a few days after New Year, Mary began to have cramps. She looked at Kate, and both knew the time had arrived. Mary took to bed and Kate helped in anyway she could. Her toughest job was keeping Jacob from underfoot. She finally told him to stay in the living room until the child was born.

At two in the morning on January 5, 1884 Mary gave birth to a son. Jacob, in the living room, heard the first cries of the baby and could not contain himself. He rushed into the bedroom to find Kate cleaning the baby and wrapping it in a soft blanket. Kate looked up as the bedroom door opened and spoke to Jacob.

"It's a boy and he has all the equipment. Congratulations."

Kate then took the newborn and gave it to Mary. Mary looked tired, but she was beaming a wonderful smile. She took the baby and held it close to her, speaking endearments to him. Kate left the room.

"How ya feelin'?" Jacob spoke to Mary.

"Tired, but just wonderful, Jacob. Would you like to hold your son?"

Mary held the baby in both hands and held him up for Jacob to take. He paused a moment and looked awkward, then reached down and carefully took the fragile package and held him in both arms. Suddenly, his feelings for a child changed from anticipation to love

Silver City

and an unspoken internal commitment to do all possible for his son.

Mary asked, "Have you thought of a name?"

"I have, Mary. I hope you agree with it, and if not, let me know, but I would like to name our son after my baby brother, who I had to give up in Oregon a long time ago. I often wonder what happened to him, and would like our son to be his namesake. Only if you agree."

"That is fine with me, Jacob."

Jacob gave Mary a broad smile. "Then his name will be Basil Deary."

Mary spoke softly, "And his nick name will be Bas."

Jacob spoke again, "I feel like a king." He looked down at Bas and said, "We will work side by side."

****

A few days passed and the new baby had more attention than the President of the United States did. Jacob watched as the women cooed and lovingly cared for the boy. He decided it was time to visit Silver City and celebrate his son's birth.

Jacob rode the black stallion to the Idaho Hotel. He took his mount to the stables down behind the hotel and walked up the short slope to the Idaho Hotel Saloon.

"Gentlemen, the drinks are on me!" Jacob called out.

The bartender spoke, " What's the occasion?"

"Mary and I have a healthy son!"

A roar of approval went up from all in the saloon. Jacob received congratulations and pats on the back. He stayed in the Idaho Hotel saloon until dark and then rented a room for the night. He rose and returned to Three Forks the next day. In his packet of surprises for Mary were chocolates, flowers, and a backlog of Avalanche Newspapers.

ELEVEN

Jake reached New York Summit, pulled his Ford pickup off the side of the road, and stopped. Slowly, he let out the clutch, keeping his right foot on the brake. The pain eased as the muscles relaxed in his left leg. It had been three years since he was shot in the back and certain situations still brought pain with full measure. Jake reached into the jockey-box and grabbed the amber pill container. He popped the cap and took two of the percocet out, put them in his mouth, washing them down with the dregs of a warm Diet Coke.

"Jesus," he spoke softly. The pain from the rough drive up from the valley left him pale and light-headed. He thought that his days of dealing with back pain and surgeries were over. Life is full of surprises. The Triumph Mine shooting had been three years ago, but the wound was still acting up. Jake wondered if he would ever get back to normal.

He opened the truck door and stepped outside. Jake straightened up slowly and reached around with his right hand to massage his lower back. He looked out over the Treasure Valley. He could see for 75 miles up and down the valley.

"What an adventure!" He spoke out loud. It always impressed Jake what heart it took to carve out a living in this land.

Silver City

The breeze blew up from the valley and across the top of the summit. This was the new road that replaced the steep, narrow road out of Reynolds Creek. Jake looked over at the juniper trees among the rocks, then up at the clear, eternal blue sky and thought how crisp and clean this area is.

He returned to his truck and began the descent and short drive into Silver City. The gravel road wound around the mountainside and then dropped into the valley. On the left Jake passed the old stone dynamite storage house. He thought how at one time this was the main road and well maintained. The road narrowed, and he passed some old, small homes on its edge, then crossed the bridge. The Idaho Hotel stood out on the left.

The old hotel looked worn out. It had a white-wash paint job that could not hide the years. The boards drooped, the roof sagged and it just looked run down. The good news was that it was still standing and in use. Jake pulled his pickup into a spot in front between two all-terrain vehicles. Three kids stood on the porch drinking pops, enjoying their new playground. Jake paused in the truck and noticed that the back pain was gone.

He stepped out of the truck and went in through one of the double doors. Inside it looked like a poorly kept museum. On one side was a glass cabinet with old odds and ends - ore samples, Chinese newspapers, and cups. The other side of the entrance hall looked like it might have been a check-in desk.

Jake walked into the dining room, and on the left was the old bar used at the Idaho Hotel. A smattering of tables and chairs were in the center of the room, and along the side wall, a case with books about Silver City and the local area resting between bookends.

"May I help you?" The balding man came from a doorway that led to the kitchen. He stood behind the cash register.

Jake replied, "Diet Coke."

"Yes." The man pivoted and went to the kitchen and then returned.

"One dollar." He took the dollar from Jake and rang it up on the electric cash register. He continued, "May I help you find something? We serve lunch and a family-style dinner." With a sweeping gesture he pointed to the books on top of the sideboard, "And we have a large selection of books about Silver City."

Jake found the man more informative than he wanted. He politely replied in a manner not to encourage any more contact. "Thank you."

Among the books Jake found a booklet with all the old obituaries in it. He thumbed it casually, and then found Jacob Deary's obituary. He closed the booklet and called back to the storekeeper, "How much for this one?"

"Five ninety-five plus tax."

Jake paid for the booklet and left the hotel. He stood on the porch for a moment. He walked down Jordan Street and up Dead Man's Alley. The shade at the front of the Sommercamp Saloon was just right and Jake went over to the porch, sat down on the boardwalk, and leaned back against the wall. The booklet was sky blue in color and not very thick. He turned to the obituary of his Great Grandfather and began reading.

March 3, 1899

DEATH OF JACOB DEARY: JACOB DEARY, who died in this city last Monday, was born at Quincy, Illinois, October 1, 1846. He came to this county in 1865, at the age of 19, and has since made his residence here, a good citizen and highly respected. In the early 70's he located a ranch in the West End of the county, in partnership with J.C. McLafferty, and since that time has devoted his whole attention to stock raising. He was married at Trout Creek, April 4, 1883, to MISS MARY MAHONEY, five children blessing the union, BASIL, the eldest, now at All Hallows College at Salt Lake City.

MR. DEARY has been ill for three years past, much of the time an invalid. Something over a year ago he went to Salt Lake and submitted to a severe operation for cancer of the bowels, which gave temporary relief, but he was given no hope for a permanent cure. In the face of slow but certain death, he maintained a cheerful disposition through all the long months of suffering, and to his wonderful nerve alone is due the fact that he was able to ward off the grim destroyer for so long a period. In December last he had a very bad attack at his home in Pleasant Valley, but through his will power, he rallied, and at his urgent request was brought to Silver City about six weeks ago and placed under Dr. Weston's care, in whom MR. DEARY had unbounded confidence. The doctor held out no hope to the sufferer, who insisted upon an operation. Last Thursday an operation was performed, disclosing a cancerous growth in the bowels which defied surgical skill. The patient suffered no ill effects, but when informed of the results he lost his nerve and seemed to give up the unequal contest, although he maintained his cheerful mien to the last. His death was peaceful - from a quiet slumber to an endless sleep.

The funeral took place Wednesday afternoon, under the auspices of the Odd Fellows, of which fraternity he was an old and valued member. Past Grand Master, Mark Leonard officiated with the burial service of the order, and despite the inclement weather a large gathering of friends were present to pay their last respects to the dead. Interment was made in the Odd Fellows cemetery with the usual rites.

The sympathy of a large circle of friends goes out to the bereaved widow and orphans.

CARD OF THANKS: MRS. JACOB DEARY desires us to express her heartfelt thanks to the many friends who extended assistance and rendered kindly offices during the illness, death and burial of her beloved husband. To the Odd Fellows, especially she wishes to acknowledge her appreciation.

November 3, 1899

A BEAUTIFUL MARBLE SHAFT has been erected over the grave of the late JACOB DEARY by his widow. The stone was delivered and erected yesterday in the Odd Fellows cemetery.

    Jake finished the obituary and decided to go see the gravesite. He drove a short distance from the hotel, turned up towards Florida Mountain and the road that leads to the cemetery. He parked a few yards from the cemetery and walked up the hillside.
    Time had rusted the iron fences, mountain laurel grew where it wanted, and runoff cut grooves between the graves. In the near corner was the marble shaft for

Jacob Deary. He knew the pain medication was making him melancholy and a bit more sentimental than he normally would have been.

A cool wind came up the valley and caught him by surprise. Jake thought that if he hurried he might be able to visit Jordan Valley and the Three Forks Canyon before dark.

****

Jake bounced and drove slowly over the old road through Ruby City and Booneville. The valley at one time used to contain large mines, elegant hotels, homes and businesses. Now, only tailings on the side of the mountains and indentation beside the road gave any hint that this had been was a working area for thousands of miners. The race track was gone, and most of the area was overgrown with willows and juniper trees.

He left the narrow valley, driving the gravel road that connected to Highway 95, and turned left onto the paved highway. Old Camp Lyon was close to this area. The land, now sparsely populated, gave little indication of what it was like more than a hundred years ago.

On the outskirts of Jordan Valley, what once was called Baxterville, Jake slowed and turned right into the cemetery. He knew some of the pioneers and relatives were buried here. Jake took a second right, parking under the shade of a tree. He stepped out and scanned the area: not a large cemetery, only for the locals, well-maintained and looking as if the residents were honored.

Silver City

Jake had been here years before, but no longer remembered where exactly the headstone and grave were. He walked up the gentle slope, through the middle of the cemetery, looking for familiar signs. He spotted a marble marker with rose colored veins, walked over to it, and was pleased that he found her grave so easily.

The inscription read: "Mother, Mary J. Deary, November 7, 1852, August 13, 1925." Jake felt remiss. He knew so little about the woman. She had raised five children. Did she keep the ranch or move to town? Was she well liked? Who were her friends? Her children lived long, full lives. Basil died in his eighties. Jake recognized how much heart it must have taken to live and prosper in this tough land.

****

Jake stopped his truck before the descent into Three Forks Canyon. He looked out at where the three rivers converged and at the rugged canyon walls. The late afternoon light caught the cheat grass and imbued it with light so that parts of the canyon wall seemed to glow. This was everything Jake thought of as the West - rugged, isolated, and wild.

On the far canyon wall, the marks were visible of where the soldiers tried to build a road. The zigzag direction of the road climbed the steep side and then stopped in the hard rock near the top.

The road down was steep and rough. In the canyon the road flattened out and he slowly bounced, driving the three miles to the hot springs. At the end of the road, he could see steam rising from the hot springs on the other side of the river. Jake removed his boots and put them in the back of the truck. He walked across the river feeling the warmth of the hot water on his legs, then climbed the short distance up the rocky bank. Jake came to a deep pool of hot water. He removed his clothes and stood naked on the edge of the pool. Jake edged into the hot pool and leaned back to let the water run onto his neck. He could stand in the deep, broad pool. Jake wanted to savor every moment. He was leaving for the Middle East again in two days.

 Jake turned his head and saw a coyote on the edge of the pool looking back at him. The coyote looked curious and amused. It turned, climbed the rocks and disappeared.

About the Author:

A.J. Lee lives in Boise, Idaho with his wife Sasha. Currently, he works as a clinician in a medium security prison. Jacob Deary and Mary Mahoney are his Great-grand parents. **Silver City** is his second novel.